# THE CREOLE
# WITCH

## Maurice Frisell

  www.trafford.com

North America & international
toll-free: 1 888 232 4444 (USA & Canada)
phone: 250 383 6864 ♦ fax: 812 355 4082

# ~ PROLOGUE ~

*Bayou Foamier was almost forgotten.*
*It was too deep in the swamp and wilderness.*
*Even at the time of Sier de Bienville,*
*it was of no interest.*

*Before 1803, the general Crescent City*
*held its own enchantment.*
*Within the embrace of the United States,*
*Nouvelle Orleans was*
*cosmopolitan.*
*Happy and proud of its wondrous social life.*
*Wickedness was a rumor.*
*Spectacular "good times" was the rule.*
*The jovial Golden Life!*

*It was not until the hungry heart of*
*urban sprawl, that the forgotten*
*bayou was rediscovered ...*
*Only to become exclusive, posh, "Bayou Gardens."*

*Velia and Michael were happy with their new home.*

*Velia lapsed into dreamy thoughts.*
*"What ground! What a garden I see!"*

*Michael sees it as just fine for his dogs to romp.*
*Maybe a fountain—a fish pond?*

*Velia held lovingly to Michael's arm,*
*—pressed her face against his sleeve.*

*The girls at work claim to remember*
*ghastly stories that their*
*grandmothers told.*
*She shivered.*
*"How silly."*

"... and they shall no more offer their sacrifices unto devils, after whom they have gone a whoring."

Leviticus
Chapter xvii, verse ii

# CHAPTER ONE

Through the deep shadowy branches of the high oaks, the honey-glow of a lighted window caught Michael's eye. He stirred in bed to make a more detailed study of his new neighborhood. The lighted window, far off in the trees, suggested the sentimentalism of an old-style lamp to him. There was something strange and beckoning about its glow that troubled him.

"What a fine old house that must be," he thought with sleepy nostalgia, "strange . . . it seems to be rising from out of the bayou waters." He patted the bed beside him tenderly, "when Velia gets back we'll walk over and see it." He curled up to the pillow, "fine time for her to take a business trip." He drew his knees up and drifted off to sleep, whispering, "Velia, I love you."

But Michael did not sleep well. During the night he had a strange dream about that old house.

Upon awakening, he immediately looked out of the window. The sun had risen high in a cloudless blue sky. Drops of silvery moisture clung to the long-stemmed stalks of grass that grew along the edge of the bayou. Something of the dream came back into focus: "There's something mysterious about that house," he murmured.

The phone downstairs rang. He got out of bed, his pajama-bottoms fell to his knees, and he stumbled. The pajama draw-string had obviously broken during the night. He quickly pulled up his pajama-bottoms, raced downstairs, and snatched up the receiver. "Hello."

"Michael?"

"Yes." He recognized the voice of Rachel, his sister-in-law.'

"What are you doing?

"Holding up my pajama-bottoms, the draw-string broke during the night. With Velia gone, I had a restless night."

"Any news from her?"

"No. I called Atlanta yesterday afternoon and she was in conference with the fur and frock committee, couldn't be disturbed. I told them I was the husband, but they wouldn't put me through to her. So, I left a message for her to call me."

"Mike, when Velia's on her annual spring buying-tour, she may as well be on Mars. Wish I'd gone with her. Meanwhile, you're coming over here for dinner tomorrow night."

"Thanks, Rae, but I can. We just moved into this place and there's un-opened boxes all over the place. I couldn't even find a pair of my pants, much less make myself presentable for your dinner guests? Besides, there's a mountain of river-sand sitting on the front lawn, waiting for me to spread it out over the grounds … got to dig a trench for the boxwood, too."

"Paul and I are dying to see your new place. It must have taken someone mighty powerful to get city officials to finally change the zoning laws of that section of town. They say that it's going to become the "Ritz of the Crescent City." Now, about tomorrow night. I don't care if you come over in your fallen-down pajamas. Just show up here! I promised my sister Velia I'd look after you while she's away, and I'm going to! There'll be cocktails, delicious roasted beef, oven-baked potatoes, interesting company . . . and, of course, my special home-made bread."

"Well . . . that does sound better than a frozen TV-dinner."

"Then I'll set your place at our table." Rachel released one of her strange, long, laughs then hung up.

"In-laws!" Michael grunted, then hung up. "That's no laugh of Rachel's—it's a shriek." He lifted his arms in a gesture of resignation which he'd often seen Rachel often do and his pajama-bottoms fell to the floor.

Spring weather was late in coming and the cooler temperature invigorated Michael, while he worked in the garden. He occasionally glanced over his shoulders, hoping his mystery house would appear in the distance, but it didn't. Turning his attention fully upon the garden, he crouched down to inspect the trench he had dug on either side of the walkway. The soil was so black and rich that he felt an urge to dig his hands into it. He shook off his gloves, scooped up a handful of the moist, fragrant soil and held it to his nostrils. He felt proud. Nowhere else on earth but New Orleans' river delta could such rich black loam be found. He let the black grains slither through his long fingers and sighed, "What wonder is the primitive correlation between man and clay."

He put his gloves back on and placed a matting of peat-moss into the trench. He lowered the balled-sack of boxwood into it and heaped a pyramid of humus about its stumpy trunk, then patted it firmly with his gloved-hands. Then he moved on to the next planting, repeating the same process, reminding himself to keep the hedge in a straight line. As he worked, he could hear the heavy drone of road-machinery in the distance. An, occasionally, the raucous talk and laughter of the work crew. He thought, "They must be cutting a new street through the woods, for the new subdivision."

His legs felt stiff, after crouching for so long. He rose, stretched his hand behind his waist, and scratched the small of his back. Unexplainably, the racket of the working-men annoyed him, "I hope those fools don't sacrifice that fine old house, in the name of progress? They don't build them that way anymore. It should be renovated—not torn down!"

On a sudden impulse, Michael decided to go see what the workers were doing.

He walked down the new, wide path which they had cut through the trees. On either side of it, they had sectioned off large plots of land sites for future homes. In the distance, at the far end of the clearing, thankfully, many great, spreading oaks trees still grew in dense thickets along the nearby, winding bayou.

With anger, Michael stared at several high mounds of wounded-greenery, lying on the ground. They seemed in pain for having been violently gouged from the earth by brute-machinery. "Progress!", he scoffed. He turned his gaze toward the bayou's sun-dappled surface, hypnotically flowing behind some bushes, out of sight for a moment, then reappearing between some tall, yellow reeds, as it flowed onward toward Lake Ponchartrain.

He stared at an abandoned bulldozer. "I see the usurpers have quit work for the day."

But from seemingly no where, a workman appeared. Michael asked him, "How's about that beautiful old house, back in the woods? Is it going to be sacrificed?"

"What house?" The sturdily-built, red-faced workman said, pushing his steel-helmet back off of his forehead and wiping the sweat from his forehead with his outer-palm.

"The one practically rising out of the bayou. I live just up the road a ways. I admire it, from my second floor, bedroom-window."

The workman laughed, "Ain't no such house around these parts, mister. Just Delta-jungle that's hell to cut through. Where's your place?"

Michael turned and pointed, "Up the ways a bit." He craned his neck to locate his house, but it was not visible. He turned toward the workman, intending to say—"I must have wandered further than I thought. The house can't be seen from here"—but the workman had vanished. Michael chuckled, realizing that he was a lanky fool, standing in the middle of a deserted work-site, talking to himself.

The sun began to set and the evening shadows lengthened. "That old house is definitely out there somewhere, near the bayou," Michael thought, "hidden amongst the folds of the bayou's thick, sinuous branches, and old, moss-laden oak trees."

The darkness of night, like a silent cloister, closed in on Michael. Everything became mute. "Well", he thought, "my need to prove that old mysterious house really exists will have to wait."

He started home, thinking happily of his wife, Velia. He wondered if she would like some mimosa trees planted by the edge of the bayou. Not only would they be lovely to behold, they would graphically mark-off the western boundary of their property. "Yes," he decided emphatically, "clusters of perfumed mimosa, shading the gloss-flow of the bayou. They would make a perfect retreat for a small pavilion. We could spend lazy summer afternoons alone there, enjoying taut lemonade and sweets, and sweet hugging!" He laughed at his romantic thoughts.

When he arrived home, the sight of the mailbox made his heart leap with expectation, hoping there would be mail from Velia. Happily, there was: A beautiful postcard of Atlanta's Peach Street, and a long, loving letter.

Lying back in his bathtub, filled with warm, soapy water, Michael read Velia's letter.

> Darling,
>
> Sorry, about your call…when the conference finally broke, it was too late to call you. Bad timing, this fashion-buying, just when we are house-moving. But I asked Rae to look after you while I was gone. I know you think she's and her friends are mental cases, but I love her. What a cook! Mike, I bought you something that you've wanted for a long time. A great fishing reel: a Garcia Ambassador. Also, a velvet,—" forest-green fishing jacket! It will go great with your blue eyes and sandy hair.
>
> Love, Velia

Michael smiled and placed the letter down upon the tile floor, next to the bathtub. Playfully, he folded the envelope into a sailboat and set it afloat. With amusement, he watched it sail down his chest, past his navel. He slithered his body deeper under the bath-water. Suddenly, he asked himself, "What did she say? 'Forest green velvet?' God!"

He quickly scooped up Velia's letter and read again:

". . . velvet, with silver buttons." He frowned, "What kind of a fishing jacket could that be?

He looked ups took a final glance out of his window on the second floor. Out there was only blackness, the whispering of leaves and stars drifting in the wind. He drew up his knees. He was really sleepy. He said: "Velia."

The first light of morning began to silver the long, wet grass growing along the edge of the bayou, great drops of moisture clung to the longer stems and glistened. However, Michael had overslept. So when he had awakened, all was still and dry. The sun had risen high into a cloudless blue sky. But he did not sleep peacefully. A dreamed had troubled him.

Michael got suddenly out of bed. When he chanced to look at the window something of his dream came to his mind. He lifted his bare toes to the window sill, got a firm, grip on the window frame and raised himself upward. There was little special to see. Sane grassy area, a clearing away of more woods, but nothing more.

"I dreamt of an old house," he murmured. He lingered on bare tip toes and meditated en his dream. He seemed to be in a spell. He forgot how long lie stood there gazing outward. Sit he grew gradually aware that his pajama pants were slipping down to low and that the phone was ringing. He jumped backwards from the window sill. Hitched up his pajama pants and went seeking the demanding phone. He remembered it was downstairs. The extension were not in. That was for Velia to decide.

"Hello!"

"Michael?"

"Yes."

"Rachael. What are you doing?"

"Holding up my pajama bottoms at the moment."

"Glad of that. What about Velia?"

"Don't know. Galled Atlanta before going to bed. Somebody told me she was out „ At a conference, A fur and frock committee. They got mad because I disturbed them „ Well, I got mad right back. Told them who I was. If they did not mind, I wanted to leave a message f or my wife."

"Oh, Mike. She must be swamped. Velia's on that big spring buying for the store. Oh! I whish I could have gone with Velia. But I am sure she will call—maybe today. Meanwhile you are coining over for dinner."

"What? I can t even find my pants. Don't know which packing case to open. Thing in a mess, here."

"Tomorrow night, About seven-thirty."

"No, Rae." He set his finely molded mouth in a determined line. "Got so much to do around here. There is a mountain of river sand sitting on the front lawn. It has to be spread over the grounds."

"Dinner at eight, my boy, I told my sister I wouldn't let you starve."

"But I want to dig a little trench f or the boxwood."

Rachael offered a merciless lure. She murmured: "Cocktails... Fine whiskies . . . Beef . . . roasted deliciously—irresistible! Baked poh-tah-toes . . . Can't you just smell my homemade bread? Other-many good things. But . . . er . . . if you can not attend—"

"What—how's that!"

"Then, I will set a chair. You will round out my—table. Beside all this. I haven't seen the place, so I am dieing to pike. Anyway, while Velia's away, Paul and I, have been talking about coming there aid giving you a hand." Rachael gave one of her long, strange laughs. "Listen, Mike they say that neighborhood is the ritz! Talk has it, that it is just too! Too! They rake their leaves wearing diamonds!" Rachael hung-up, laughing at the top of her lungs, "See you, brother-in-law."

"Michael put down the telephone. Rachael's laugh still rattling in his ears. "That is no laugh," he said. "It is a shriek." He mocked her. He forgot, too, that one hand was holding up his pants. He lifted his arms in the manner like Rachael, and this time he lost his pajama bottom.

An hour later, Michael stopped his work and rested on the handle of his spade. He looked back at the house. It's outline of white brick. A moment later he crouched down to inspect the trench he had dug on either side of the walk way. The soil looked so black and rich, he felt he had to put his hands into it. Shaking off his gloves, Michael scooped up handfuls of moist fragrance and brought it to his nostrils. The wonder of its substance went to the physical and spiritual essence of him. Nowhere else, can earth be found such as that like the black delta loam of New Orleans. He allotted the crumbled black soil to slither through his long fingers, with a sigh he thought: There is something to this. This primitive correlation between man and mud.

He placed a good matting of peat moss into the trench, then put down the balled-sacks of boxwood, heaping a pyramid of humus about the stumpy trunks then patting it down with his glove hand.

He went on to the next.

All the while Michael worked he could hear in the far away distance the heavy drone of a tractor and road machinery.

The loud voices of the road-gang at work; the harsh raucous of laughter.

"That must be where they are cutting the new street," said Michael, "making a. new subdivision."

He rose to his feet. One hand rubbed his back. The muscles in his legs felt stiff. Also the loud racket of the machinery and men annoyed him. Suddenly it occurred to him: "I hope those fools are not planning to sacrifice that fine old house in the woods!"

On an impulse Michael decided to walk over and see how the new street was taking shape. The road gang had cut out a deep wide path through the trees but could see nothing of a house of any kind of structure. There the street was being formed, some of the land had been cleared and staked-off into log for suture homes.

[cannot read] reading oaks grew in thickets on the far side of the cleared area. To the left wound the bayou.

Michael looked so the cut and wounded earth. It looked to be somehow in pain, being ruthlessly bulldozed, coerced and violently intimidated by brute-like machines. [cannot read] trees whose once lovely limbs had been remorselessly broken and heaped aside. He looked about the distressed progress.

His eyes scanned the wooded area. He reached the sun-dappled curve of the bayou. {cannot read] sight of its [cannot read] behind a blind of bushes, but quickly sighted it again amid some yellow reeds. [cannot read] Lake Ponchartrain.

[cannot read]. But [cannot read] for the day.

[cannot read] house back in the [cannot read]? Asked Michael with a smile.

"What house?" relied the red-faced man. He wiped his forehead on his sleeve. He pushed back his helmet.

"Why, that old place bade in the woods," Michael positively replied. "I can see it from my second floor."

"What?" laughed the red faced man. "Ain't no house back there, podner. Only jungle, It is a killer just to get through— Where's your place?"

"Right there," said Michael, but he suddenly had to break off and wonder. He could not see his own house. How could he have wondered so far? He turned to face the man. But he was gone.

He paused somewhat bewildered. It was an extraordinary scene to Michael. He realizing himself, a lank figure, alone in the middle of the broken earth and tumbled branches. The high trees closing him in like a cloister, blotting out the sky, and not a breath stirring a leaf. Silence smothered everything. Evening shadows began to lengthen.

Michael took another swift look around and began to retreat. He felt certain that there was an old house whose window shone from within the folds of the sinuous bayou and through the moss laden branched of the oaks.

"It's got to be in there!" he said. He thrust his hands in his pockets and strode away, wondering if Velia would like some mimosa trees by the edge of the bayou. It would mark off the boundary of their house. "Yes!" he cried, "I think some mimosa with its perfumed clusters shading the glass flow of the bayous would make a nice retreat for summer afternoons. Velia would like that. And a sweet place for hugging!" He laughed.

Once back at the house his heart quickened at the sight of the mailbox. There were two beautiful postcards and a long, loving letter from Velia.

Michael lay back in the warm soapy water of his bathtub; there he read and re-read Velia's letter. He placed it down outside the tub. He picked it up once more. Randomly Michael scanned the page.

'Darling, sorry about your call . . . Conference did not break up til an awful hour . . . too late to call you . . . Bad timing, this fashion buying just when we are transferring houses . . . Did my sister call? Help? I know you think Rae's a mental case, but I love her. What a cook! Mike I bought something you've been wanting. A Reel; Garcia Ambassador . . . Also a jacket. Velvet! In forest green. It will go great with your blue eyes and sandy hair . . .

Michael placed the letter on the tile floor. He reached up and released the warm water. He turned on the cold water to full force. He discovered that the envelope had fallen into his bath. He caught it before it got too wet, then expertly folded it into a little sailboat. He slipped dfown into the water. he watched the little paper boat float past his chest; past his navel. He slithered deeper under the water. The flowing water kept getting cold! Cold! He felt the pink of him turning icy-blue. Suddenly he shot his head and shoulder out of the water. He caught up Velia's letter. "Did she say, velvet? God!"

'. . . Velvet . . . with silver buttons . . . Can't wait to get home . . . love, love . . . Love! . . . V.'

# CHAPTER TWO

Rachael and Paul lived in the Garden District. Rachael referred to their home as: "A modest mansion. Not big, really."

The house faced St. Charles Avenue, where on the grass of the neutral ground the St. Charles streetcar growled past on tracks that were as sleek as platinum. The gardens, the great mansions, the diamond glitter of beveled-glassed doors, the ironwork, all stood unassailable under boughs of aged oaks that lined the thoroughfare.

Michael paused under the roofed portico. He pressed the ivory button beside the sparkling glass door. Waiting, he glanced back at the avenue. A streetcar went gliding toward the universities; on the other side of the street a stream of automobile lights went flashing by. Trees and leaves and shadows went flying by in the singing evening breeze. He looked down at his polished black shoes. In doing so he leaned closer to the door. Behind the doer he could hear voices in chatter and the soft notes of a piano.

Once more a sudden wind caught the trees and shook them wildly. Once more another streetcar flew past in wrought-up tardiness toward Canal Street.

Michael gave the ivory another push. Finally when no one answered, he boldly made up his mind to admit himself. He looked down at the gleaming brass handle that was fashioned in a fancy scrolled design. He placed his thumb to the down-press and gave the door an inward thrust which almost resulted in bumping the colorfully dressed figure behind its sparkling glass.

It was Rachael.

"Michael," she cried and put toward him her long fingers. "I told them that should be you." She smiled. Her black hair was brushed out from her temples; her painted mouth racist. For a moment she postured there looking very much like a mannequin. She was dressed in a blue and gold hostess gown that trailed her ankles, a sash tucked in her tiny waist and about her shoulders she clutched a white chiffon scarf. She looked marvelous standing there and looked so much like her sister Velia. Only Velia was not so willowy. Finally she said: "What detained you?"

"What detained you!" He barked. "The wind was about to carry me off."

"My little family party got out of hand," she whispered. "I had an unexpected telephone call. Now, we have two extra guest."

"I feared you might be up to something," He answered, "That's why I wore my poor navy blue suit."

"Bosh! You looked wonderful. Men! All they need is a shave and a tie."

"Is that all."

Great and wild happy chords of music came flooding in upon then as they whispered. Michael recognized the melody but could not guess its composer. He leaned his ear toward the music, his face a little puzzled.

"Puccini!" Cried Rachael. "This is the part where Butterfly is so wild with delight. And how the Contessa can play."

"W-Who—?" Michael gagged on the question.

"I told you I had a telephone call my dear Contessa Lucrezia Millano Zinadelli, and her niece Betty. As you know . . . or rather don't know, Mike, her niece Betty attends Dominican College. Tomorrow evening there is to be a recital at the school."

"And?"

"And, that is how and why Lulu is in the Crescent City." Michael was not certain, but he thought he understood all Rachael said to him. However, there was no time to think for Paul appeared in the vestibule. He planked a highball into Michael's palm while at the same moment Rachael drew him toward the great room just off the vestibule.

A young woman was seated in the depth of a wingchair and the Contessa was just rising from behind the shining grand piano.

"This is my handsome brother-in-law," said Rachael, drawing him toward the tall handsome woman.

Somewhat shy and feeling a little awkward, Michael bent toward the Contessa Lucrezia Millano Zinadelli, She, in reply, gave Michael a rather long and investigative smile. She was fashionable dressed. Two or three strands of pearls wound about her throat. A diamond broach there snapped out its brilliance in blues and scarlet fires. Her hair was beautifully arranged. It was cut in a style that was known in former times as a boyis-bob.

Her eyes were gray and penetrating. However, Michael's eyes were equally discerning. He smiled: "C-Contessa . . ."

"My gracious!" The Contessa retorted. A short laugh heaved her ample bosom. "What has this wicked girl been telling you!" She flashed her eyes upon Rachael. She extended her hand to Michael's and caught his fingers strongly. "You just call me, Lulu, young man," her voice was warm and throaty. "My friends do."

"But a Contessa? Should I?"

"First; yes to that. And, yes, I am that. It is true," she went on. "But I must put you straight. I am Contessa Lucrezia and all of that . . . but only because my family kept strict records and documents of our family linage. Our blood line goes back to Pope Clements time. You know in those time Italy was a prolific maker of counts." She waved her arm in an extravagant gesture. "Every Italian Prince . . . from the Pope downward created them. for love or money."

"But Aunt Lulu," chimed in Betty, "please tell Michael that was over a hundred years ago!"

"This is my niece, Betty," replied the Contessa. She motioned to the young lady seated. She was in her twenties. Quite pretty. A cluster of soft brown curs curved at her neck. Her eyes were large and wide apart. She couldn't seem to keep them away from Michael.

"Betty is accurate," she said. "Over a century since grandsire and his forbearer abandoned such. They fled to America, escaping with their lives and a fortune, such as it was. They were finished with feudal and petty kings. Louisiana called them! So you see young man, all this really makes us simply something like Italian-Cajuns." She finished with a breathless and shy laugh.

"So you see," explained Betty, "we are simply Americans after all."

"That is quite a whirlwind of history," said Michael, "but I think I understand it all. All right, I will call you Lulu." He squeezed her hand. "But maybe I should have worn my velvet."

"Rachael told us so much about you," inserted Betty, "I wish you could come to my musical recital tomorrow evening at Dominican. Aunt Lulu promised me I could were the crown jewels."

"If I can find them, Betty," the Contessa declared. "I think I put them in a shoe-box." Suddenly she swung about and went on in her rich throaty voice. "But, Rachael! You said nothing of this young man's aura. He has a beautiful aura. I read aura, you know?"

"Yes, Mike," answered Rachael from under the archway. "Lulu is wonderful at things like that."

"Oh, decidedly . . . decidedly! There is a distinct atmosphere surrounding your being Michael. It is about your head. How well I see it!" She turned silent. She drew within herself. She was so deep in thought she pulled her lower lip.

Rachael intervened. She said, the table was ready and from somewhere in the dining room, Paul was ringing a little silver bell.

From far back beyond the pantry; the wonderful aroma of homemade bread assailed Michael's senses. He felt suddenly starved. His eyes encountered Rachael's.

"Yes." she nodded with a big smile. "I made it myself." Then in her friendly and beautiful fashion, Rachael tossed her head gaily. "Dinner . . . Dinner, everyone!" She danced off to the dining room. Paul was there. She took his arm.

Later. Much later the little party discovered themselves in a quaint and well appointed den at the rear of Rachael's little mansion. Paul went about refilling stubby shaped glasses with apricot brandy.

The Contessa waved her drink aside. "Paul, is it your intent to get and old lady drunk. Shame." She struck out at him with a playful slap. She picked up a dish of nuts and chocolates. "The diner was wonderful, dear Rachael. But I could not keep this up. I'd lose my matronly figure."

"Rae," said Betty excitedly, "During dinner, Michael told me he is faced with the most extraordinary mystery."

"What mystery is that, Mike?" Rachael asked.

Michael twisted his head toward Betty. "I don't know what she means," he stumbled. "Unless she means Velia?"

"I understand Velia is on a buying trip for the store," observed the Contessa. She was drying her fingers on a napkin. "I should have gone with her," replied Rachael. That lucky girl." She faced Betty. "I don't think Mike is going to tell us anything about his mystery . . . so I think you better tell us, Betty."

"Really. I have no mystery," said Michael.

"Yes you do!" laughed Betty. "You told me there is strange house in the woods near your place and it disappears!"

"Now, this is the second time I've heard of this," Rachael observed. "Remembered? You mentioned it to me over the phone."

"Oh, did I mention that over dinner?" asked Michael. "That shows how talkative one can get over a good dish of food."

"What's this?" Questioned the Contessa gravely. A piece of chocolate was paused at her lips. Her expression, her somber voice gave a peculiar chill to the moment. At that same time, the little clock on the shelf struck the quarter hour, and a sudden prolonged wind howled about the house; it then made a passing sound dawn the chimney. The incident seemed to have taken them aback for an instant. They looked into each-other's faces, then laughed.

"Spooks. I guess." someone murmured.

The Contessa clasped her hands in eagerness. "Really, Michael you cannot keep this to yourself. Tell us! I knew I read something special in your aura. How, I know I am correct. Tell us of this phantom house."

"There is nothing to tell. I know it must be there in the woods. I guess I simply can't find the right way to get to it. That's all."

Rachael said: "But Mike, didn't yea tell me the other day you went looking for it, the workman told you that there was nothing back in the woods."

"Yes"

"But you see the lighted window from your second floor bedroom?"

"Yes. But after a little while I can no longer see it."

The Contessa was simply absorbed: "How baffling! You mean it simply vanishes."

"I think it is creepy," Betty rasped. "Strange."

"Not strange. Not creepy, either," asserted her aunt. "We have all heard of the house of Loreto."

Michael looked back at her, "I don't think I knew of the house of Loreto?"

"The Holy House of Loreto. It is common knowledge. Tradition has it that the house wherein the Holy Family dwelt at Nazareth, was transported by angels to the city of Loreto."

Rachael drew nearer. "Isn't that something."

"One may see it today. Since the 13th., century to our present day it has been a holy shrine to the Blessed Virgin . . . Maybe, Michael, that this house, that you see is also of the supernatural." She gave them all a sudden and grave look. "and, I think it is."

"Oh, Aunt Lulu," Betty moaned. "You turn my blood cold."

"Indeed." she glanced at her niece. She turned back to Michael. "I caution you, my young friend, do not think me a foolish old woman. I have studied with the Rosicrucian for years. The aura is not to be taken for naught."

"I don't know anything of the aura," replied with a faint and shy smile on his lips. "All this mikes me feel a bit stupid. Phantom house, aura and angels."

"Now, you must not be cross with me, Michael. The aura, is that eternal emanation from one's psychic. Our souls, you might say. That special light associated with the spirit form. Really. You have aroused my concern, Michael."

"I am not cross."

"But you'd rather not hear."

Betty saw her moment to speak. She interjected an unwanted remark. "Aunt Lulu says, that half of the housed in St. Martinsville are ghost ridden." Her aunt lifted her head, then turned a pair of scathing blue eyes upon the girl, but she talked on. "Longfellow says it is the Eden of Louisiana.

"Michael raised his brows: "[cannot read]"

The Contessa nodded: "Our ancestral home is there."

Michael saw his opportunity to have some fun and teased her. "And . . . I suppose your family home is simply overrun with spirits. The psychic and angels . . ." His breath rippled into a soft laugh. "Maybe, demons, too! Lulu."

"Why, you naughty upstart!" She broke into laughter with him. She shook a finger under his nose. "That is my point. But you will not give me credit. These days, it is said that there is not a single demon in hell. Hell is emptied of all evil spirits—and they are roaming the earth." She grasped his hand warmly. "Now, listen. Be careful, Michael. Your aura warns of peril. In the near future." She tightened her grip. "Take this warning seriously. Please!"

He squeezed her hand in return. "I don't mean to be rude. I'm sorry. I will be careful, if it pleases you."

Rachael rose to her feet. "You better listen to her Mike. Lulu, knows! Ohooo, goodness!" she pretended to tremble. She drained the last drop of her brandy. "Such talk. You people give me goose-flesh."

"Me, too," Betty said.

Once again the antique clock struck the hour, but this time, the lateness reached out at them, and sped each into a whirlwind of departure.

"Good Lord!" Cried the Contessa. "The time! I am telling you," she said, in a shrill voice, "if Betty did not have that recital at Dominican tomorrow . . . I would come right over to your place, mister. I'd get to the bottom of this business." Her hand primped at her hair. "Oh, how my own psychic admonishes and counsels me. Indeed. Lulu knows what she speaks of."

Moments later they were all jammed into the vestibule. Betty was whispering something and giggling as she held on to Rachael.

The Contessa Lucrezia Millano Zinadelli was wiggling her shoulders into the swirl and voluminous folds of a Chinese shawl. Her jeweled fingers flashed as she drew up the fringed edge to her throat.

Paul was standing quietly at the opened door. A swift draft of spring air came sweeping along the floor, chilling ankles.

Michael felt the Contessa's hand touch his pocket. She had quickly dropped an object into it. Her hand patted down the pocket's flap, "Hold on to that," she cautioned in her low, throaty command. "You may need it." She planted a troubled kiss on his face. She walked away in rapid steps.

Betty followed.

Rachael, seconds later, placed s package into Michael's hands. A brown bag. It felt heavy. The pack held with it the aroma, of meat and warm bread.

"You may get hungry later," she said warmly. As she walked him out, she was laughing. "And, remember hew Lulu warned you. Forget that nutty house." She giggled. "Wait til Velia get home."

[Cannot read] "Lagniappe for me. Gee! Thanks, Rae."

Rachael giggled again. She almost tumbled and place her hand on his shoulder.

"Rae," he inquired. "Can you be tipsy? "Or, me?"

"Paul," she responded. "He thinks we are tipsy."

"Nice party, Rae. Thanks."

Paul reached out to Rachael taking her into his arms. As the door closed and the key rasped in the lock, could hear her soft laughter.

# CHAPTER THREE

He drove directly home. He sped down St. Charles Avenue, easily, almost traffic free, at that hour, down to Canal Street to City Park Boulevard. He found the trip surprisingly quick. Michael also went directly to his bedroom, but trekked quickly downstairs again to secure the locks at the windows and doors.

"Lulu!" he grumbled half amusedly. "What guff!" He went about searching his bureau draw. But so much conversation would not leave his mind. "Angels and demons—and, what did that woman say?" He questioned. "Oh—? My aura." Michael suddenly laughed. "She saw my aura . . . humph! I wonder if that was altogether decent? She said: 'my aura was in future peril'. "New what does that imply?" Finally is discovered what he wanted in the draw. "Here they are." he pulled out a fresh pair of pajamas, or at least the bottom half. The pants was soft white and possessed a good dependable drawstring. He pulled them on and secured the cord. "Wait til I tell Velia about my aura." He fell upon his bed, but not before he took a last look out of the window and dark whispering woods beyond.

There was no lighted window. No house.

He would just lay still awhile. He flexed his toes. He allowed his thoughts to drift. A smile took possession as he thought of Velia. She would laugh. Such nonsense! Velia would never let Michael forget. "But, Mike! you are seeing thing."

He longed to reach down and draw up the covers. He had intended to do just that. However, fatigue over powered him, and Michael with night-bound eyes went meandering into a nether-world of sleep.

From somewhere out of the blackness, Michael heard the magic sorcery of a woman's laughter. His eyes strained the darkness to see. The young woman was unknown to him. However, he could sense that she was rushing away. The frantic clatter of her silver heels suggested that she might be fleeing in terror.

She stopped running; under the street lamp she paused to replenish her breath. There, under the glow of the street lamp, Michael observed that she was simply beautiful. She was full bosomed and was wearing something purple. There was, too, a misty glitter about her dark, swarthy head. She glanced over her shoulder and gave Michael a long, studied look. How hearty she seemed. The worldliness of her smile suggested such intimacy that felt shamefully affected. He turned away, for he could no longer look at her.

In reckless derogation she flung her dark head backwards and laughed at his shame. Then, nervous and high-spirited, she turned on her silver heels and ran away down the empty polished street.

Michael rushed a few steps forward to search for her. But the mysterious woman had simply disappeared. Too baffled to go on he paused in the shadowy gloom and listened. All he heard wad the dank dripping from the roofs. The dwindling of hollow laughter; and in her wake wafted the faint scent of perfume. He could taste it on his lips.

Then he saw something!

There on the drifting wind floated a lavender scarf—Chiffon so soft it seemed to have no strength or substance. Something suggested that he look upward. The sky seemed curiously foreboding; it was faintly flushed with long fingers of fire. The moment closed-in on him. Michael felt a sense of loneliness. It crept over him, smothering his heart.

Once again he glance upon the sky. Now it was smoldering in deepest flames of crimson. Its fire began to devour the clouds, boiling them in passionate scarlet, foaming into bluish-red, then to impenetrable blackness until he could no longer see.

Michael stumbled along, fearful, lost and wandering. Suddenly, up head out of the blackness, he heard the tapping of a walking-came.

Soon the turbid obscurity began to lift. A voice then whispered: "Hello there! So . . . it is you, Michael?"

Michael clicked his slips to reply, but his throat was too stiff to speak. The figure slowly began to creep up from, the darkness, and his heart found a moments relief. He recognized the race at once. It was Contessa Lucrezia Millano Zinadelli.

"It is Lulu!" she admonished. "Don't you know me, man? She lifted her thin hand. The jewel on her crooked finger splashed brilliantly.

"Uhh? . . . Lulu!"

"Yes, yes" She rasped out of the gloom. Her gaunt features appeared waxen in the struggling lamplight. "I told you, Michael your aura is in peril! You didn't believe me. You scoffed at demons. I warned you to beware. Again I say beware! These days there is not a devil left in hell. That arch-fiend,

His Satanical Highness has set them free to roam. To menace the earth."

Lulu grasped Michael by his coat lapel and drew him, with unexpected strength, under the dreary, splintering light of the street lamp. Michael began to wrench away her tightening fingers. But he was forced to stand and listen. Her eyes pleaded that he should comprehend the importance of her words. Then she relaxed her grip. She saw that her words had reached, him.

He paled. All life seemed to have drained out of him. There were taut lines about his mouth and chin, and the terrible anxiety in hid darkly blue eyes was no nice to see in a face so young.

"Good Lord!" He sighed. Then through half-closed eyes, Michael allowed the hideous suggestion of demons to flash across his brain.

All at once he pulled sway from her presence and began to run without direction down a blackened path. It seemed he was racing across some great open expanse. Now and then he stopped and peered back to see if anyone or anything was following. The wind began to blow in a strong fit of agitation. Up ahead he spied a faint glowing. Cut of the dull illumination, he once again encountered Lulu. He question how ever, did she get before him?

"What's this you say about a house?" The wind began to blow harder as she was creeping toward him, hair-bent against its force. She pulled at her fluttering shawl. "You say: A phantom house in the woods? Believe it! . . . You think a house does not have a spirit . . . You think it does not dream, too? It dreams in the twilight for a wooded grove. It longs to be loved . . . Think it just stone and wood? Its doors are songs. Its doors await for those for those who have departed. It languishes, wanting them back. Of time you house is good. But evil can abide in you house. Evil! Beware, too, that you in your innocence take into your house. Many come with sweet-face and dainty-footed—But be watchful of them. Michael, I warn you . . . ."

Afterwards, walking in a deep dark silence, Michael heard some one cry. It was more like a scream. It sounded like the voice of a young man, but the agony of which, Michael had never before heard. It was if the man's soul lay in a final battlefield between heaven and hell.

It was if the world was tumbling and falling in space without sense or direction. Then the old mansion in the woods loomed out of the blackness. The old house seemed to move; he saw it clearly before him.

But instead of Michael peering at the house. The house was spying upon him! Somehow the bulk of it had drifted up to his very own bedroom window. It was like a thing alive. It posed a kind of spirit. It weakened Michael.

The lighted window looked at him as if it was an awful, living eye. He held his breath and waited. The awful light waited, too. It seemed to have wanted something of him.

Soon out of the stillness there came a sound of rushing wind. Upon its sliding breath, Michael heard the madding sound of stomping hooves. It drew nearer until for a second he thought the wildly beating hooves would run over him.

Suddenly, Michael as if to escape his terrible predicament, shot up from sleep and the ghastly quandary that took possession of him.

He awakened to find indeed that the wind was blowing at rough and high peregrinations with the night, and that it had found the side wall of the house and the trellis, and the sticks upon it were rattling like dry bones.

But who at that hour of morning was riding astride a horse. For he did here the dull thud of hooves, But the room was too cold for him to think further. He trembled. He needed his pajama top. But he could not find it at the start. However, there half-lying across the chair was his shirt. The onyx and diamond link glimmered in the starched white cuff. He thrust his arms through its sleeves. He shook his head to free himself from whatever he dreamed. He rubbed his brows. He gave a few slight moans of relief. Suddenly, Michael felt the need for lights. He began to switch them on as he walked. He unthinkingly began to walk down the stairs. "Oh, yes," he said. He recalled what he wanted. The care package, Rachael had slipped under his arm was on the table, waiting.

Michael realized as he buttoned his shirt up to his neck that he was simply starved.

# CHAPTER FOUR

The following morning brooded on the verge of heavy rain. Once a smoky sun glowed through a haze of grey clouds but soon vanished. It was evident that the dismal dank had crept in to stay the day.

Michael had gone out on an errand, and returned home sometime around four o'clock. He remembered that there was a pair of antique side-chairs that Velia had urged him to pick up for her. He had just taken the chairs from the trunk of his automobile, and put them down safely into the hall when the telephone unexpectedly sounded.

The cheerful ringing simply pulled him eagerly down the hall. He reached the little table and gingerly grasped up the receiver.

Breathlessly he said: "Hullo . . . ?" He thrust his fingers through his hair. It was dank from the drizzling rain.

"Mike, honey!" Velia said the bright voice.

"Velia! Thank God. I had a hunch it might be you—or hoped. My gosh! Woman, I think 1 could have got through to Pope more easily."

"Gee, honey. Don t be mad."

"I'm not mad, V."

"No? Then is why is my end of the 'phone smoking?" Velia chuckled.

"Well, V . . . I left enough messages."

"Gee, honey. I'm sorry. This place is a crazy house. How are you?"

"O.K. I am bringing in chairs."

"Aunt Bess's antique chairs. Mike, how do they look? I hope she gave me the gold velvet pair.

"Yes. They're gold. A little drizzle fell on them. The sky is about to fall down here."

"It is beautiful here. What are you doing?"

"Bringing in chair. I just got back. I went to the office to get the blue-prints on the weaver project."

"I thought you were off?"

"Yes. It was the lunch hour. I picked up what I needed and beat it out of there before anyone knew I came or went—When are you coming home?"

"No later than Friday. I promise, Mike."

"Well, thank God, yes! I want to see you V . . . if you know what I meant."

"I want to see you, too, darling . . . And . . . I know what you mean. Have you been eating . . . Did you go over to Rachael's . . . I don t want to come home to a hairy skeleton."

"Rachael gave a dinner party. Velia? Do you know a woman—oh, what her name?"

"No, Mike I don't know, What's-er-name . . ."

"Don't be funny. She's royalty."

"Royalty! Rachel knows royalty?"

"I met her at the party, A real spooky ole girl—Oh? I remember . . . her name is Contessa Lucrezia Mil—"

"You mast mean, Lulu! Was she at Rachael's . . . ?"

"Say, that right—Velia you know her . . ."

"Lulu is momma's girlhood chum. They went to school in France."

"Some friend, momma has . . . . She says out loud that she can see my aura." Michael could, not restrain his laughter.

"Now, who's being funny, mister?"

"Well, that's what she said. At the party. In front of everybody, too."

"But, Mike . . . Lulu is wonderful. We love her."

"Well, i think she is spooky."

"Don't tell the ASPR that."

"What that . . . a new political party?"

"Michael, that is the American Society for Psychical Research. Lulu set the world on edge in 1944 when she wrote her book: The Invisible Presence Among Us."

"Velia! Here I am, a man alone . . . No woman to protect me, and you're telling me about spooks. invisible ones."

Velia began to giggle.

Michael continued: The ole girl said, she saw my aura . . ."

"Mike . . . stop playing. This is long distance."

"You not worried that she saw—"

"Please, darling . . . I must go. I have an appointment with our fashion designer, Juillota in two minutes."

"You said you'd be back when—?"

"Friday . . . But I will call again . . . love you, Mike . . ."

He lingered for a time with the buzzing receiver in his hand. For a moment, Michael thought he heard something stir. It seemed to have come from the back rooms. He waited but told himself, it was only the weather. When he lifted his eyes, he discovered, to his surprise his own face reflected so white in the mirror on the opposite wall.

Then there appeared: The mysterious phenomenon of lightning! It came as specter catching him unaware, it flickered at all the windows, pressing for entrance then silently vanished. It left him somewhat transfixed in the gloom of the lonely ball.

Outside he heard the unexpected beat of hooves. Its muffled thuds flew past the house. He frowned. He said to himself:

"But there is no stable in the vicinity?" He was certain.

Michael replaced the receiver. He went about his affairs. He checked the front entrance. He looked out. The weather had turned to a wet, shadowy haze. It blurred the trees and shrubbery; so that sky and earth seemed like a poor charcoal drawing. It also occurred to Michael that the house was set-back a good bit from the road. He asked himself:

"How could I hear a rider . . . hooves? He wondered in dull recollection: "Where have I heard hoof-beats like that before?" He had obviously forgot his dream of the previous night.

He backed way from the unpleasant weather, when he had closed the door and snapped the lock, Michael was crossed with the notion, that something was stalking him. He gave a quick glance about and laughed at himself.

It was an unfortunate remembrance that he heard Velia's voice telling him: "She wrote: The Invisible Presence Among us."

"Ha! Tell that to your nanaine!" scoffed Michael.

He could not imagine just what made him dredge-up such an 'old-time' expression. He hadn't heard it in years. It was typical, Old New Orleans.

It caused him to recall his aunt, who ironically was his nanaine.

"But, Aunt Ernestine has been dead for years." Michael walked off toward the dinning-room. "Maybe I ought to have a drink?" He discovered a beautiful crystal decanter. It was half-full with brandy. "Invisible Presence Among Us . . . eh? . . . Could be the old girl's got something there?" He pour out a good dram of the golden liquid. Then he pour out a little bit more. "I think I need it," he said.

A little while past 8: p.m. Michael retired to his room. He brought with him a small volume of Teaddale's poetry.

Once there his thoughts turned to the house in the woods. In fact, thinking about it was beginning to be a part of his day. That afternoon, too, whoa his restless spirit urged him out to look over the grounds, and saunter down to the bayou, he found himself looking for it. But the weather was simply too dismal for him to see very much or far. However, Michael enjoyed tramping about in the wet and foggy weather. It was one of the favorite thing he like since boyhood. On wet afternoons, as he returned home from school, he would deliberately scud through puddles and gutters. To walk under dripping branches of green and bronze leaves. Nothing could be more delightful. Rain and rough weather lent interest to the otherwise ordinary.

Fully dressed, Michael lay down upon his bed. He tried to read but his thought would not stay with the page.

> Listen, the damp leaves on the walks are blowing,
> With a ghost of a sound;
> Is it fog, or is it rain dripping
> From the low leaves to the g round?

". . . As if I don't know it is wet and dripping without," he muttered lazily to the book and laid it aside.

He got up went to the window and pulled aside the curtain. He looked out, but nothing seemed to be out there in the wooded dark.

The only thing visible in the glossy window-pane was Michael's own reflection.

He reasoned: "Maybe if the room was in darkness, he would be able to see better." He turned out the lamp end returned to the window, but nothing awaited him that he had not seen before. He questioned if that elusive ivory light, which played so much upon his thoughts and compelled his attention was simply something he imagined.

"No!" he cried in agitation. "I have not imagined it. I saw it—sure!"

Then he recalled the words of the foreman of the road-gang saying: 'Ain't nothin' back in them woods, podner . . . it's a killer just to get through . . .'

Presently another explanation came into his thinking. "Could it be that I am seeing swamp-fire?" he asked himself. "No, no," he disputed. "The evidence of these last two night is just too positive." Suddenly he clasped his hand to his forehead. The recollection of his dream came back to him! "What was it I dreamed?" he rasped. "My God! This is insane. Why am I so impelled toward this . . . this . . . ?"

Suddenly it happened! An unexpected burst of lightning flashed and brightened the sky. And he saw it! there it stood!

Not merely a house—But a mansion!

There were gables and dormers. A high pitched roof. 'There was a on one side, a tower. There was, too, that very questionable window.

"Ah!" Michael rasped. "You do exist."

Suddenly he spun around. He thought that a presence was near, and had touched him. He felt that a terrible affliction had taken possession of him. He thought he had heard a voice. That from out of the woods it called to him.

He began to tremble as a malediction of anathemas fell from, his lips. Such vile expletives; such oaths arrested his soul. Swearing was not Michael's custom.

He turned from the window; slowly he gathered his jacket from the chair. Silence earns to take possession of everything. He held his breath. He bent forward to listen; Did he, once again, hear the dull, distant thud of hoof-beats?

Michael's blue eyes were glazed. They took on a wild and curious chinning. He felt he must go out. He was determined to solve the mystery of the house that was . . . And, the house that was not.

# CHAPTER FIVE

Michael paused in the middle of the newly cut street and looked back. He wandered if any of his neighbors might have seen him stealing towards the woods? He could see the freshly laid asphalt. A wooden road block barred the way. Here and there black iron tar-post glared their light against the night and wind. He walked along the shoulder of the road. The warm glow of the burning tar-pots lighted part of the way. Their orange flames reflected against he trees, but beyond their glowing, lay darkness and the wet stillness of the woods.

He regretted the he did not think to take along a flashlight, but not going to return to the house. He wanted to go on even though his judgment warned against his rashness. He felt he must find his objective. It occurred to him that if there were a house, there should also be a path.

His fingers struck the side of his trousers.

"Of course!" he exclaimed, realizing that attached to his keys was a small flat pocket light. He got it out and beamed it just ahead of his footsteps. Beneath his feet, the ground felt solid, much firmer than an undergrowth of weeds. He stomped his feet. He crouched down, and pulled away some tufts of grass. His fingers began to probe the ground beneath the wet roots. The discover of his touch sent a thrill through him for his fingers met the cold touch of stone.

"There is a path!" he whispered. He felt as if a force was urging him deeper and deeper among the thickening trees.

Without Michael realizing it, the path turned. Then it turned again unknowing to him that the woods had silently closed behind him. He continued onward with the feeble light of his torch before him. He heard the sound of the rushing bayou slithering through the reeds and mossed draped trees. The gurgling sound was a guide to him, he felt he could make his way along that. Presently-smooth stones began to show themselves under the tangled overgrowth.

Soon up ahead his light picked up something, which caused him to freeze in his tracks. It caught the blurred shape of a small furry creature. Michael crept nearer to the questionable white figure.

"A cat!" he cried in great surprise. "A little white cat."

He called to it, begged it coaxingly for it to draw near. However, the small cat only mewed. The cat stood in the path, boldly obstructing the path like a sentinel on duty. It gave another mew, seemingly to warn Michael, The cat blinked its luminous green eyes, sat upon the path and curled its tail about its haunches.

Gently, Michael reached his hand to the little animal. She pushed her moist nose toward him; she snuggled her head onto his palm. She purred as he scratched beneath her chin. Soon she pulled away, and that was the first and last time she allowed Michael to pet her.

There was a low growl of thunder and lightning suddenly scrawled across the sky.

"It is going to storm, Kit . . . And, one of us was not smart enough to bring rain gear. I think we are in for it."

The little cat began to thrust her soft body against Michael. He reasoned that the cat was using all of her strength to push him back. One gift that Michael prided was that of loving and understanding animals. However, since the passing of his last pet, Wendy, he had denied himself that association. But he knew that animals, whose minds are free of complicated patterns of human thought, are the perfect receivers of the Master Mind's signs and manifestations. Such imminence as the invisible, evil and death aroused their gifted sense and warn of the fact.

"Are you warning me, Kit . . . ?" he murmured, looking upon the cat as a guardian-spirit. "I don't understand . . . must I go back . . . ?"

Her tail began to wag violently. She growled. She rubbed against his trouser leg. She rose upon her hind legs and pushed, emitting a low, ominous ululation.

The cry suggested such terror that it seemed to change the course of Michael's blood. The cat fixed a warning stare upon Michael and never wavered in its gaze. The little animal growled again. Afterwards when Michael's bewilderment finally passed, he stammered:

"W-What—Kit!"

All at once the wind rose. Lightning and thunder crashed out in pandemonium. It menacing force shock the surrounding world. It tore the heavens, so that its electrical-flashes intimated the man and the animal at his feet.

But there, before Michael, in the stormy flashes, he saw the house!

He found, himself standing just a few yards in front of the towering iron gated. Surmounted over its pointed iron-spears, curved an elaborate arch of iron-lace. In its fancy scrolls and workmanship were set the letters:

## FOURNIER

Michael could only lift his head and stand before the gates in wonderment. As he paused in long thought with his lip fixed between his teeth, he felt as if some force had taken him and left him spellbound. He could only wait for his spirit to return to him as the storm gathered, and the leaves and wind lashed at his body.

At long last, he cleared his throat and spoke the name: "Fournier." Looking through the iron bars he could see the magnificent edifice brooding in the storm. How desolate and secretive it looked amid the somber cluster of evergreens, meaning in the wind.

He realized himself been drenched by the rain. He scurried for shelter under a nearby oak but found it totally unsuitable. When next Michael turned his attention toward the mansion he discovered that somehow the gates were now standing open to him.

This latest discovery gave him quite a turn, and at the same moment, Velia voice sounded in his head: "The Invisible Presence Among us"

"That all I needed to think of just now," scoffed Michael, trembling in the rain.

He glance at the lane leading to the great place. It stood mute and powerful under the tumbling rain. It was a blend of Grecian and Victorian elegance, styled perhaps for some eccentric. The side facing him boasted a high, wooden tower with little balconies smothered in ornamental iron work in the Creole style. The first floor had long French windows, all tightly shuttered with long green blinds. A long gallery ran across the front of the house with beautifully proportioned Doric columns.

Only later did he see that the gallery floor and the columns were rotting and grey with neglect. Wet to the skin, Michael searched the foreboding depths of the gallery for the front door. Although he was unable to see the door he made a bold run to the house and up the granite steps.

When having reached the shelter of the gallery, he saw the door was deeply recessed, almost hidden under a low hung balcony. He turned to look back. By now the grounds had flooded until they were almost and extension of the bayous itself. The house was evidently constructed in the deep U of the bayou, for Michael could see the stream of it curving up and embracing the building. He scanned as much, as he could and wondered as to where the cat may have gone?

Once again he sought the aid of his flashlight. He beamed it on the entrance. In the double front door that were set into mahogany panels, Michael saw a pair of raised initials. The letters: C. F. gleamed in the sparkling glass. He leaned forward slowly tracing his fingers over the letters. But soon he was startled. Surprised that a light was beginning to press against the glass; that the door had open silently upon him. He stood amazed and blinded by the glow of a kerosene-lamp that was being thrust into his face! The burning fuel rose to his nostrils He could taste the oil. Its film touched his lips.

The lamp's flame began to smoke against the wind. Its light revealed and aureoled the slight figure of the mulatto-woman behind it. She stood erect, stiffed lipped and contemptuous of Michael's presence.

"Who be dere?" The woman impudently questioned in her French-Haitian tones. She placed her hand upon her hip, glancing suspiciously at Michael. She spoke in a low, throaty voice. "And . . . What you want here, M'sieur?"

Michael felt quite guilty at having been discovered at trespassing. In a guarded, humble voice he replied: "Pardon . . . miss . . . pardon . . ." he found he had to raise his voice in order to be heard above the heavy rain. It was obvious to him that the woman was displaying airs. There seemed something unnatural about her. Also, she seemed to be wooden. And although Michael was often tease about his small ears, they were keen at detecting, beneath her airs, the woman's Gumbo-patois. "I had to take cover under your gallery," Michael went on. "I was walking in the woods . . . Do you own a cat?"

"Humph!" came her incredulous grunt. She stepped closer to Michael. She lifted the lamp. The light fell upon his face, and the bedraggled and soaked appearance of him. The woman's amber eyes narrowed into slits as she looked up and down the length of him. "Humph!" "Dis is Fournier house," she stated with pride. "Madame Camille stay here . . . I t'ink wedder not too bad, M'sieur. Go!"

The woman delighted in her treatment and dismissal of him. She backed deeper into the entry. She waited for him to leave. Now, the lamplight fell upon her. This gave Michael a good moment to look back at her. Although she was not young, she did convey an appearance of false youth. A kind of astral-knowledge touched Michael's mind. It instructed him that this woman seemed to have been of another age; that although she walked, she belong to that which was both ancient and desiccated. She was dressed in black silk. She wore about her thin shoulders, a large handkerchief-like scarf. Her small head was swaddled in a glossy tignon of black taffeta.

For a long moment, her burning yellow eyes met his. A spasmodic movement quivered her throat. She restrained herself, seeming to be biting back a perilous warning. She savored the horror or her delivery and whispered dryly.

"It was not wise to come dis night to Fournier House!" She stepped back. She began to close the door. "Bon Soir, M'sieur."

# CHAPTER SIX

"Mimoutte! Mimoutte!" A woman's voice aged and shrill called from somewhere down the long passage.

The yellow Haitian stopped the door. She twisted her head over her shoulder, and the golden hoops of her earrings glinted in the lamplight. She listened again to the calling voice.

"Allow the gentleman in! Commanded the severe and authoritative voice. "Admit him, do you here? . . . And, I thank you to mind your place.

Mimoutte cowered. She bowed her head and stepped aside. "Enter . . . M'sieur . . . Poor servant will show you to Madame."

"What?" interrogated Michael. His voice almost lost in the wild rain. He was being thrashed by the storm. "Am I to be admitted!"

She bowed her grudgingly, stepped aside, lightning Michael into the entry. A stale smell of dust clung everywhere, especially when the woman pulled aside the heavy folds of a velvet curtain and led him into another somber, high ceiling passage. Mimoutte and her wavering lamplight went before him. Her long skirt caused her to glide effortlessly. To Michael she seemed to have floated. Because of the poor lighting it was hard for Michael to see very much on either side of him. He felt that the passage made an unusual long walk. He followed her blindly observing that they passed-by a number of heavy curtained doorways.

Suddenly he grew conscious of a strong fragrance. He began to inhale it again. At first he could not recognize what the smell could be.

Mimoutte paused and looked back. "You like, M'sieur?"

"Oh!" gasped Michael. "Oh!"

It was the sweet burning of incense. The entire passage was laden with its cloying perfume. When he took a fresh breath he could taste it. Its savory sweetness lingered in his throat. It was liken to opium. Never had he known such a taste! Searching for its source, Michael saw just to his left a large bowl. It was fashioned of a purple glass and holding some kind of oil. Suddenly the bowl burst into flame. Its light fascinated Michael. He stopped spellbound. He felt that this strange woman had somehow willed the bowl to flame.

Mimoutte smiled in a most idiotic way. Her yellow features assumed an idolatrousness expression that for a moment Michael felt she had totally lost touch with reality.

The bow of oil began to leap into higher and higher golden flames. Its rich light grew brighter and brighter until Michael saw just exactly just what lay before him.

The trembling fingers of fire were warmly embracing and sweetly caressing a gleaming brass image. A Fat, Monstrous body of a toad!

The sight of it stifled Michael. To him it seemed like a shrine. An Altar! As indeed it was. Fixed deeply into a recess that looked like a curved pyramid sat the gleaming image. It rested on a wide legs of black marble, about it in a semicircle was place a number of small golden pots.

The storm outside stopped and everything was so unusually silent. Michael felt that the world he knew had crumbled away; that the only tangible existence was this circle of gloom, this strange creature with her lamp, and the flames adoring the ghastly golden icon.

Suddenly a kind of phonetics, which were madding in their delivery came from the Haitian's strained throat: "VEE-KEE-NO-O-TEE-EES-RAWN..." She began to gather dust from the various bowls and sprinkled them into the high, trembling fire. Then once again she repeated her horrid cry. There was something about the very tone and sound of her cry that began to repel and sicken Michael. "Him! Him!" she crooned, It sounded as if she was saying: 'Heeemm...Heeemm' Her eyes smoldered, she turned upon Michael.

She said in a raspy whisper: "Isn't it wonderful, M'sieur? Your eyes are privileged to see such! You do like Mimoutte," she urged. Her thin fingers caught Michael's hand. They bit into his flesh; they felt like talons. She forced him to follow her immolation. "See..." She pressed his hand into one of the golden bowls of dusty herbs. A horrid dry laugh rattled in her throat. Mimoutte was delighted at having involved him into the sacrifice. She laughed even more as he infuriately snatched by his hand.

Michael recoiled from the icy feel of her arid skin. He tried desperately to wipe off her touch. He felt he had brushed death.

Mimoutte turned glassy-eyed, she seemed in a trance, withdrawn and mindless. Her tongue hung over her bottom lip. She looked like a yellow, insipid monkey.

The next moment she seemed herself. Michael wondered if she had pause to hear, for he himself had the notion that something he could not understand was creeping toward the house. The stillness was broken by the rustling of her dress for Michael saw that she was groveling before the image, and began to pinch-up different herbs form the bowls.

"This . . . Senna leaves! Old time Creoles say it good to staunch blood. Bad blood . . . This filet-powder . . . wonderful!"

Her thumb began to grate against her fingers, sprinkling the mystical dust about the altar. She deposited a heap of powder on either side of the toad.

"This is Aloe! Aloe!" she chanted. "It is alleged by the wise to expel melancholy from the soul . . . make you forget dead romances." She continued to dispel about an odorous gum from the East and sweet smelling roots. "And . . . Hovenia dust. Yellow like gold . . . Said to turn men mad with passion!" She put some hovenia dust into the hollow of the toad's belly. Its smoky perfume began to rise from inside the creature. It drifted out from the vacant eyes and gaping mouth. The wispy vapors rose upward out of sight and soon filled the passage until Michael felt he would feint from the heavy aromatic balms and fragrant spikenard wood. "Ancient people love spikenard . . . Good Charm!"

Suddenly as if she suffered a change of mind, she got between Michael and the altar. She shielded the altar with her narrow back. Her amber eyes saw Michael's amazed expression. She pointed her toe making a dancing movement. She sang, forgetting the flaring lamp in her hand, and almost tipped it over. She smiled unpleasantly showing the broken slant of her teeth. She delighted in her own cruel amusement.

Once more her face changed to an expressionless mask. She turned to the alter gathered another pinch of herbal incense and deposited it into the toad's belly. Suddenly this gathering of herbs began to burn. The flame rose and pressed lovingly against the toad's body.

Soon another incantation came out of Mimoutte. But this one was not the Gumbo-French which she had heretofore spoken, nor the soft patois Negroes had developed in their effort to speak the pure French of the aristocratic Creoles. This dialect which Mimoutte uttered was neither English, French, or Gumbo. It was not like anything spoken by men under God!

She turned back to her Gumbo speech: "Come, M'sieur," she said softly, and added contemptuously: "Madame Cecile wait f'you."

Just at the moment she placed into the toad's belly exploded and sparked upward. When Michael flinched, he suffered the embarrassing feeling that Mimoutte was laughing at his Baffled innocence.

"Quite a side-show," he lashed back.

She took him further down the passage. He was relieved to get away from the smothering vapors. Mimoutte too him to a heavily curtained doorway and left him there alone.

"Regrettable weather, my young friend," said an aged, trembling woman's voice from the other side of the curtain.

"I was walking in the woods," said Michael. "I got trapped in the storm. I had . . ."

"Yes, the rain. But it was inevitable that is should storm this night . . . this night!" she repeated. There was a quality of emotional suffering in her voice.

"This night?" inquired Michael.

"You will know later, Michael."

"Madame knows my name?" he said astonished. He waited for the curtains to part, or a request from Madame for him to enter.

"Pity! Pity!" she went on. Mimoutte should not have detained you in the weather. It is not gracious. "Although her high-pitched voice quavered with age, it revealed the cultured quality of an aristocratic.

Michael cleared his throat. He felt sure by now she would entreat him to enter. He leaned closer to the musty draperies, "I apologize for having disturbed your household," he said. "Your servant seemed so very cross with me, Madame ..." He ransacked his memory for her name: "Fournier ...?"

Waiting for a reply, Michael turned his attention back up the passage toward the shrine. The silky vapors of incense were slithering from the toad's gills while the flames flickered in adoring worship before the strange icon. The shadow of the thing trembled its fantastic in dilated proportions upon the wall.

Bizarre and ancient instincts struck at Michael's heart. The fine hairs on the nape of his neck stirred.

"It is ... Satanic!" Michael overheard himself say involuntary. The thought haunted him as he stood amid the drifting vapors and heavily scented aromatics. The lonely moment troubled his brain as he trembled wet and uncomfortable in the silent corridor.

Never could he recall himself in a more awkward situation. He was in a strange house, poised before a musty curtain conversing with a host that did not invite him into the room, nor gave no reply to his questions.

Lulu's voice invaded his thoughts: "Now-a-days there is not a demon left in hell ..."

Michael wet his lips and tried again. "Madame . . . knows me . . . ?"

"I am not Madame Fournier," she replied at long last. A certain amount of revulsion colored her voice. "No, indeed! I am, Madame Du Bertrand, but am usually called Madame Cecille. And," she balked, "Mimoutte is not ours . . . Mine and Jacques. She is, Camille's. Mimoutte is Haitian. Camille in her travels, found her in the wilds of Martinique—Heaven forbid!—Camille brought her here to Fournier House. Jacques and I would never have her. That one is too full of gris-gris, and island superstition." She paused. ". . . And, you are called Michael."

"That right. But I don't recall meeting . . . You have the advantage . . ." Michael wondered why she did not ask him in. "How do you know my name?"

"Now you are behaving like my Jacques," she said in gentle reproval. "The young ask too many questions of the old. We do not like to answer. We are tired. Jacques is young, also. But the important thing is you are here!"

"That I am. In all truth it was the glow of your lighted window . . . I saw it from my house, through the trees . . ."

"How can that be? There is no other property for miles around. The Fournier estate covers all these surrounding acres. Ask, Jacques—Oh! Oh! Poor Jacques my poor boy!" Growing sorrow overtook her. Her voice suddenly broke on a high sob.

Michael heard her weeping. We put his hand to the curtain. He started to pull it aside, but changed his mind.

"Is Madame all right . . . !"

"Pardon, Monsieur . . ." Her restrained voice, caught all restrained tears so very audibly that she coughed. Her breath seemed stifled. Then, evidently she collected herself, her syllables took on the beautiful clear Parisian tones while she stated an old proverb from the Louisiana Teche country: "Chacun sait ce qui bouille dans se chaudiere ... eh, Monsieur?"

Michael labored to assemble his poor French. Translating: "Everyone knows what boils in his own pot." Michael blinked and waited for a long silence passed between them. He muttered under his breath: "Exactly just what is boiling ... And in what pot. What goes on here!"

All at once in abrupt, concern, Madame Cecile exclaimed: "Poor boy! What have I been thinking of? You are soaked to the skin. How thoughtless of me!"

"I will be all right, Madame." However he was wet and trembling.

"Mais non! Not another word. You mast get out of those wet things . . . now, you know better. Take the tower stairs to the first floor. It is Jacques' room. You will find the door ajar. Mimoutte will take care of your clothes while you wear something of Jacques'. . ."

Michael waited, but not another word came from behind the curtain. Madame was unaccustomed to disputes, and evidently she had spoken her final word. He appreciated her hospitality but had no intention of going up the tower stairs, nor, removing, as she said, his "wet things". He waited a moment more, hoping and expecting that she would come out past him. Surely she must. However she simply did not. In final impatience, Michael forcefully drew the heavy curtains aside and entered!

The room was empty!

Not only was no one there, it was simply devoid of furnishings. A solitary chair, however, had been drawn up to the fireplace, beside it, on a low marble table rested an elaborate oil lamp.

Under the great arch of the mantelpiece, a log fire smoldered for breath. Its feeble fire outline and accented the blackened andirons, which were fashioned, for some purpose, in the figure of a toad.

On the hearthstone, with forepaws thrust before it, lay the white cat Michael encountered in the woods. She cat turned to look at him, then went on languidly licking its paws.

Michael felt directly drawn not merely to the cat, but to the welcoming warmth of the fire, feeble as it was. Dank to the flesh, he made his baffling search for Madame Cecile and her mysterious disappearance. At that moment he felt the need of human contact, just as much as he needed the fire to halt the deep chill inside. He glanced back over his shoulders to discovered that he had made foot-tracks in the dust. Dust which lay so unusually thick on the bare floor, that if anyone, or any thing would have crossed it, certainly make an imprint. Surely, even, dry silken slippers worn by a light wraith of a person would have left impression.

But there was none, except his own. No so much as a cat's paw!

Michael felt that the room had wavered beneath him, or so he thought. But it was only this new and suddenly additional shock that tilted his world and left him cold and heavy with breath. He tightened the rein of his reasoning and looked about. He faced the cat, who quietly returned its gaze, for the cat, to him, seemed to knew confidently the answer to all his questions. She seemed to know the seething confusion spinning in his head and much more. How wise and knowledgeable she looked.

"What., Kit?" He bent toward the cat. He was surprised to hear how hoarse the raspy sound of his own voice through his constricted throat. "Why are there no prints? How did you get in . . . And, Madame out?

He saw a faded tapestry hanging en the wall to the left of him. He went over and drew it aside, thinking that it might conceal another door, but there was no opening; the only door was the one why which he entered.

The cat suddenly emitted a piercing cry. Michael thought it sounded, alarmingly like a warning . . . to go, go! Her great jeweled eyes, green as chrysolite, and flecked with gold, were gleaming, She fixed them meaningfully upon Michael.

"Yes . . . Kit . . . I know you are my friend . . . You've got to help me! Wasn't, their a lady in here. Just who in the heck did I talk to . . . She had to be sitting in this chair!"

He stepped over to the chair where Michael assumed Madame Cecile must have been sitting. Crumpled on the cushion lay same sort of soft white material. Michael picked it up; he saw that it was a gentleman's evening-shirt. An embroidery-hoop was fixed just over the breast-pocket. Angry fingers had torn threads from it! Madame Cecile must have been painstakingly at work. For a kind of design had been ripped out of the cloth.

A deep impression had been left on the pocket. Michael touched it and the few black threads that remained. What had been emblazoned over the pocket, in black silk, was the emblem of a toad. In its place where the image had been was now a white cross. Madame's needle and thread, with its white silky skein, with sudden abandonment, was thrust in the left arm of the unfinished cross.

When Michael lifted his head, he saw that the cat with great knowledgeable eyes, had been observing him.

"Yes, Kit . . . I think you know more than you can tell. Tell me, what strange lady was embroidering here. Why had she given me so baffling an interview? Who was I speaking to Kit . . . Or what was I speaking to!"

Just then, a gust of wind came hissing down the chimney. A long broke, sputtered, then crumbled into flame. It so frightened the cat that she suddenly arched her back. Her fur rose to a stiff ridge to the end of her tail. Her eyes caught the spasmodic light of the fire. She stared at one corner of the roan. The hypnotic odor of incense drifted into the room. Its fragrance was like a place of death.

"What, Kit?" Michael twisted his body. He peered into the shadowy corner. "What—!" He turned back to the cat. "Wonder if you know this little limerick, Kit? He recited:

"Cross-patch, draw the latch,
Sit by the fire and spin,
Brew a cup, drink it up,
Then invite the Devil in I"

To Michael amazement the little cat growled. Certainly, he thought it a response. His own eyes glittered. He questioned: Could his poem be in conformity with that he suspected! He sensed the cat's foreboding, but was baffled and entrapped in the dark wonder about him. However the gentle little animal had taken his heart. He felt in someway she must be a guardian-spirit, because more than once that feeling welled-up in his soul.

Once more, Michael probed the shadows, but he saw nothing.

"Scared?" he asked softly. "Me, too, Kit. A little. But would be a coward to turn back. You—think?"

He rested the shirt on the back of the chair. A sound on the other side of the curtain attracted him, and he went back into the hall. Once there, Michael felt an uneasy moment of isolation. He found himself alone and in view of the loathsome idol.

Hearing something rustle, he jerked his head toward the sound. Far above him, a light was drifting down the tower staircase. The light stopped on the landing. It was Mimoutte. The light began to waver. It drifted down one or more steps then stopped. Mimoutte affected a superior stance above Michael there on the stairs. She held her amp to one side and glance down. Her yellow face gleamed in the light. She directed in a dismal voice:

"Come, M'sieur. I show you, yo' room . . ."

Michael's upturned face returned the woman's hard look. "I think . . . maybe not," he said stiffly. "He saw her features as they tightened into an ugly grimace. Her mouth a sharp line.

"Suit yourself," she shrugged. "It is of no matter."

"AS you said, 'maybe weather not so bad'."

"You know best . . . but by now, the bayou has overflowed its bank . . . But . . . er . . . . Maybe?" she questioned with sweet malice, "Maybe, M'sieur has had the good foresight to carry with him, servant and pirogue? All ready the rain is up to the gallery!"

"Meis oui," Michael returned smartly as a bitter chuckle warbled his throat. Then a saying of his Aunt Ernestine's flashed into his mind: "Ta finess est'cousne de fil blanc—"

Mimoutte understood; she came back with a sharp parry to his arrogance. She hissed back the translation: Also to you, your shrewdness is sewed with white thread . . ."

Suddenly the sound of the storm came between them. It fairly shook the enormous old house. Mimoutte accidentally leaned too far to one side for the lamp began to flare and smoke wildly, almost plunging them into bewildering darkness!

The cat cowered and snarled. Its ears were laid back in fear; its eyes glaring horribly in simple hatred of Mimoutte.

She looked back at the little animal without one bit of human emotions. She righted her lamp, and stiffly turned up the stairs. Her hips swayed in a surprisingly fashionable grace as she lifted herself upon each step that was in a style of another time.

Michael trained dubious eyes upon the shadowy stairwell. Its banister was thickly hung with tapestries and rugs. The stairs made two sharp turns at the angles of the tower, after that, he could see no further. He waited for a long second below stairs. But soon the storm struck again in torrential madness. His blue eyes blazed in troubled speculation. He would die rather than admit fear, but felt forced to swallow hard.

A sudden break of thunder placed wings on his heels!

He resolutely skipped up the stairs.

# CHAPTER SEVEN

"You're too kind," Michael sang. There was sweet venom in his voice. He place an open palm over his ribs, giving a taunting bow to Mimoutte after she had lighted him to his door.

For by the time they had reached their destination, she had become more resentful. She whipped the door open for him to enter, then banged it shut on Michael's startled face.

He waited a second, gave the door the slighted crack and peeped through the opening. He saw her departing shadow, drift off and crawl along the papered wall.

Michael grimaced, muttering aloud: "She's got to be an accoutrement, trailing some bedraggled Mardi Gras Parade." A nervous little laugh moved throughout him. However, a warning came from the depths of his soul, admonishing him to beware of this—this? He groped for a word. "—this thing!" he whispered. Suddenly that chance remark caught fire in his brain. He held tight to the doorknob as the horror of its reality stabbed at his heart. He held his breath as in retrospection questioned his own thought: "This thing—?" From the surrounding darkness, a passing paralysis of terror came to lay-cold hands upon him. "But w-what?" he stammered, "What is she?"

After a while he pressed the door shut, and saw that there was neither key nor bolt under the knob. He sought a straight back chair and dragged it up to the door, end there propped it securely under the knob.

Michael turned his attention upon the room's interior. It was just as vast and high ceilinged as the one below. The tall, gaunt windows were heavily masked in velvet draperies. As he had first observed the old house had predated anything modern. Above his head, an interesting old-fashioned oil lamp hung from the papered ceiling. From its tarnished chimney and frosted bangles streamed a mellow light.

A great four-posted bed predominated the room.

"God!" thought Michael, "The things looks like a catafalque . . ."

Among the other pieces of heavy black furniture were a huge armoire and a chest at the foot of the bed. The only comforting thing was a tremendous fireplace with thick burning logs. The mantle was shoulder high and lovely, hand carved from white marble. But as Michael went toward it, he was troubled to see a replica of the shrine below stairs. Candles lighted either side of a gleaming image of a toad.

Michael set his teeth. He was determined to ignore whatever manifestations these ignominious idols honored.

He gave his attention to his immediate needs. He shivered in his wet garments. He could feel his shirt sticking to his skin. A sudden notion flashed in his head that he should leave. Get away. His foremost thought was warmth. But he had hardly stepped up to the glowing fireplace when once more, the rising of the storm forbade that he should leave. The wild sound of the weather filtered through the walls. He could hear the shutters trembling in the gale, creaking on their ancient hinges. Rain lashed out, blinding the windows; the high cedars moaned in the wind.

His thoughts turned back to Madame Cecile. "Madame is right," he murmured. "I am soaked to the skin . . . Madame disapproved of something . . . She was crying . . . I've got to find out," he murmured. "But how did she know of me? She called me Michael—And! These rotten shrine all over the place—loads . . . Toads? On that shirt?" he recalled, "She was embroidering a cross over one of the things?" Michael shook his head. "So what? So what? I am all wet . . . believe me, in more ways than one." He shook his head again. "How did she know me? She acted as if she expected my coming." He moved closer to the burning logs. He tried to rid his mind of his troublesome thoughts as he took off his jacket and tie. However, before he took off the rest of his clothing, he took another glance about the room. He had an urgent need for privacy. Also, he could not get it out of his head that he was being watched.

"Oh, well . . ." he sighed aloud, adding: "Michael, you've got to be out of your mind. How did you get into this! For Pete's sake! What would Velia think of this?"

At long last, after another glance about the room. He stripped, He almost lost his balance. For he tried to take off his pants over his sodden shoes. He dried his hair. He wiped his body with the towel Mimoutte had hung by the basin. For a moment the firelight played over his body as he toasted his naked self by the flames.

He saw there was a gentlemen's black silk dressing gown place across the bed. But he rejected that. Jacques name was embroidered over the pocket and about it a toad.

He searched the chest at the foot of the bed. There he found a soft white blanket; trembling with cold he wrapped it about himself.

Michael placed his shoes on the hearthstone with soles upturned for drying.

Presently, fingers began to drum on the other side of the door. A voice spoke through the paneling. It was Mimoutte.

"Madame Cecile has ordered that you should give me your wet things, M'sieur. I will dry them."

"Oh . . . all right," Michael answered, feeling exposed and awkward in his nakedness. He stepped barefooted to the door. He had to take the chair from under the knob, hold the blanket about him, open the door a crack, then hand his wet things to Mimoutte.

"Uff! Foolish man," Mimoutte scoffed when his blanket slipped to his hip and he desperately caught it up. "Give me t'ings. I see nuttin', M'sieur!"

And, Michael having excitedly about out his hand to grasp the slipping blanket, his fist accidentally gave Mimoutte a slight punch. She snatched the wet garments. "Madame see you soon, hein?" She and her flickering lamp soon drifted away.

Michael closed the door. He gave a quick look at his body. He echoed Mimoutte's remark. "'I see nuttin' . . .' Gee, how flattering of you, ole nightmare!" His arms stretched out the blanket, then drew it tightly about his form.

Something suggested he crack the door and spy upon her. She stopped midway up to the passage and dropped his clothing on a chair. Then she went a different way.

Michael leaned out a bit further to view her movements. Her lamplight seemed to be floating upward. Obviously she was climbing another staircase.

"I wonder! Could it have been the tower window lighted from my other place?"

Stealthily, he pressed the door shut. He was aware that his toes were burning with cold, while at the same moment, a Cajun colloquialism of his Aunt Ernestine's came into his memory. It was because of Mimoutte's image that he recalled it.

"Une zireté[1]," said Michael.

He raced back to the hearth and flung himself into the big chair before the flames.

A smell wineglass, and a crystal-decanter of Medina were conveniently placed on a low table beside the chair. Michael, gratefully procured and sipped a glass of the ruby-blackness.

He lifted his glass to the flames, the light of the flickering fire, melted through it. He wiggled into the blanket thinking of the strange household he had entered. He thought of his situation, that here he was, bare as a rock, wrapped in a blanket. "I just can't believe I'm here," he told himself. He sipped a little more of the wine's sweet blackness.

A low laugh moved throughout him, shaking his shoulders and rippling his belly.

Wine end comfort from the storm was very welcomed, but he knew he must consider his general position, this house and its relations to him. He immediately liked and respected Madame Cecile's gentle voice, but even she presented a mystery. She had slipped away like smoke.

"So, obviously, this Jacque's room," thought Michael. "What of him—And, of all the many rooms, why had Madame assigned this one to me?" he couldn't forget Madame weeping and the meaning of her embroidery. "Another thing!" he raised

---

[1]    A hideous thing.

his voice, "what normal person would want to look at the image of toads?"

"Presently he lifted his sight; squatting indignantly the gleaming monstrosity seemed to be glaring back at Michael from the mantle shelf. He felt that the answer to his question lay somehow in the mystery of the toad.

He recalled Made saying: ". . . It is inevitable that it should storm this night." Mimoutte has said something similar. What could be so particular about this night? He wondered about Madame's cryptic French. What was boiling in whose pot?

A surreptitious breath of wind began to disturb him. It rose from nowhere and swept about the room. I see eddies fluttered under the blanket, reaching for his skin. He looked quickly at the window, expecting that one had blown open, but no, he was mistaken. It grew into a breeze and began to rattle the fancy frosted bangles of the oil lamp above his head. The wind gave it rough shake until it sounded like bells. Soon it blew out the flame. Except for the firelight and candles he was in darkness.

Michael sensed and unexplainable weakness creep over him. His arms and legs felt heavy, immovable. He desperately tried to raise himself from the chair but couldn't.

Horrible apprehensions struck at his mind. His heart thumped in rapid beats. He tried to take a deep breath, but even his lungs were not functioning properly. He could only gasp.

For a long while he sat stone-like in the chair. An icy sweat films his face and body. He tried to control his thinking; to try and understand the uncanny paralysis that had overcome him. Had the wine been drugged—or poisoned? Something, whatever it was—was holding him immobilized.

Once more Michael lifted his eyes to the mantle. The slim candles on either side of the toad were not only lighted, but flickered being the bloated figure in such a way that its monstrous shadow loomed over the greater part of the room.

"Damn that thing!" cried Michael in a grimace of horror.

The wavering black silhouette of the toad dance over him. By some sinister force, it came alive! It's head swayed. It's throat throbbed. It's gleaming round belly began to heave with breath.

Michael tried to cry out, but his voice came only as breath. He could only sit and watch as the things ugly thin lipped mouth curved downward in an evil, reptilian-like grin!

Slowly, the toad's sleeping, almond-cut eyes opened!

The creature fixed its gaze upon Michael. Michael tried to tear his glance from that fixed stare, but it seemed but it seemed impossible to do so. Then the mantle seemed to sag, until the center of the shelf seemed to be lowering itself into the flames.

There amid the tongues of fire, the toad was seated right before him. It held Michael's gaze until he felt spellbound by the eyes. Soon the toad began to leap and cavort in the flames, melting until it was little more than a fiery lump of molten metal.

The room. The very world slipped into darkness. Transfixed, Michael could only look into the fire. As he watched, long, lovely arms with graceful hands beckoned to him. The outstretched palms offered gifts. Jewelry and chests were held up in the flames. The chests tilted toward him spewing before his feet glittering gems and gold.

With a cry Michael longed to turn away, to thrust from him, the obvious evil in the proffered wealth. But he could not break the spell which held him.

Up from the smoldering fire he could see worlds beyond worlds. He saw men and women, embracing each other in the most unrestrained of pleasures. Lust and want and luxury was everywhere. Not only could he hear their wild laughter, which was intimidating in its wickedness, but he could also feel it. It seemed to shake the very room. Nothing was denied. This was a kingdom where sin was the most exquisite of delicacies.

An insidious suggestion came into his mind. It whispered: "all this can be yours."

Michael felt that the very strength of his character had weakened, that he could not resist the seething abomination around him. He was filled with depraved desire and strange yearnings. More and more he felt drawn to look upon the lecherous debauchery.

Up from the smoke and fire, a shape arose. This dark figure of a young man. The other figures, still licentiously writhing, faded. The severe outline of the man grew clear. The amber and umber flames curled about his nude lacerated body. He seemed torn with suffering. His head was thrown back in torture in despair. His eyes only blackened hollows. His hands were clenched before him, but suddenly he flung them upward. His dark eyes were pleading. Terrible cries were wrung from his bloodied lips.

Michael looked on in frozen interest. The licking flames swept over the pain-filled body, then was soon blotted out. Instead there instantly appeared cities and temples beyond the art and imagination of any architect. Splendid cathedral-like edifices spiraled upward and beyond sight. The buildings seemed to soar on enormous wings. Space swelled and amplified. Michael felt his mind flying past time into absolute infinity.

Then with a sudden reversal of sensation, he was struck down! Down and down! Into chasms where sunless pits dropped below depths and depths.

The sickening feeling of falling was magnified by the pounding blood that rushed to his brain. He felt there was never future hope of ever escaping from so unfathomable depths.

Gradually, the pounding became soft. It now had a gentle measured rhythm. To his relief, the sound was the gentle soft breathing of the sea. He listened to its low murmur. Gentle water was bathing his feet, lapping against his ankles.

Michael found that he was naked. He was strolling on a smooth beach beside the water's edge. He relished the occasional waves washing against his ankles. There was no moon, but the sky was bright with stars.

He lifted his arms, relishing the caressing wind against his body. He felt in perfect health as if he were being shown the unlimited joys of life. The palpitating sea breeze might have been hands upon him. He felt he could lift himself on the very zephyr if he wanted. He thought, too, that he suddenly the hidden purpose of all things. The very mystery of the universe. However, the instant he learned, the very instant he forgot. Meaning was simply too vast for his memory to hold. Knowledge came, but neither did he know what, or who whispered meaning of the mystery of life to him.

Then, gentle startled, Michael realized that he was not alone!

A young woman was walking beside him. She was naked as himself. Their eyes met. Without speaking perfect accord was theirs as he stretched his hand out to the woman. Her eyes declared:

"Michael, I am yours."

She was in his arms, pressing herself to him. There were in the balmy wind. They were in the sea . . . tumbling body over body, swimming and submerging, curving together in and under the warn waves. Her long hair tangled about him, lashing his mouth and body to hers.

For a long while, Michael and his perfect, but mysterious companion, lay in repose upon the Band. It was a time, as perfect as creation.

Slowly, an elemental rumbling began. It was foreboding, angry and malevolent. It crept out of the surrounding peace to shake and shatter their tranquil accord. Suddenly the sea began to brood. It rolled and raised, then crashed in measured thunder. It banished both companion and love.

Then, Michael was too aware of another storm—Another danger. He felt himself alone and unprotected. It was if he was past the rim of the world. Then he found himself running breathlessly in the storm. But he was gaining no passage in his labored strides, realizing the dread knowledge that he was being pulled back to that awful room.

The storm rested and diminished, and Michael was slowly aware that he was again seated before the fire. A good fire, now, giving nothing but warmth and comfort. When he gained complete consciousness, he was aware that something had crashed.

The warmth livened the blood coursing through his body; tentatively, he tried too move his arms and legs. He found peace as he realized that the force which had held him wad finally broken!

Michael bolted out of the chair. His first thoughts were remembrances of a dream. A dream intermixed with terror and ecstasy too. But above all, a deep feeling of loss was his. At the core of these vaguely recalled images, was the solution to everything that had confronted him. Much of it was s blur in his memory. He shook himself back mentally. He also shook himself physically.

He looked about the room. He prepared himself for any new development, The bangled ceiling lamp had been lighted, and was simply pouring down its mellow light. All things innocent and as should be.

A low growl made him start!

It was the cat again, He was happy to see her, However she was troubled. Her ears were drawn back end her tail switched fearfully.

Michael saw that the toad was not in its place on the mantle. The candles were leaning lopsidedly in their holders and smoking. He moved a bit and accidentally stubbed his toe hard. He quickly looked down. There! Lying sideways on the hearth was the brass toad.

The cat was also glaring down at the gleaming object.

Michael picked up the object. He lifted his arm upward and back; he was ready to hurl it through the nearest window. However, he controlled himself and looked at the heavy chunk of metal in his hand. "Maybe it is best not to antagonize this—this—household?" stammered Michael. "Not if I am going to find out anything about them." He knitted his brows; "I am determined to do that," he murmured. "He looked into the fire, thinking, that he was determined to discover the mystery and malignancy within those walls!

He began to turn the gleaming object within his fingers. He hefted it in his palm. As he studied it, a long, low breath of amazement whistled through his teeth.

"Why . . . the thing is not brass. It's gold!"

While he examined the golden toad, he also understood just why made it fall.

"You, my little friend," he said to the cat. Her great green eyes were shining, her black pupils a deep well seething with strange knowledge. She fixed her gaze on Michael. "You swatted it down—Deliberately! You know. You broke the spell that held me. Thank you, Kit. You are my ally. What of Madame Cecile . . . is she a friend?"

At that moment he heard something fall or slip down on the great dresser and mirror behind him. He turned to see, but all appeared normal and still.

When he turned around again, hoping to give the cat a grateful pat, she was gone. For a moment he looked around for her but she was no where to be found.

He then grimly replaced the golden toad on the mantle. The long delayed chill and shock took hold of him. He wondered how the cat got into the room in the first place, and just who entered the room to relight the bangled oil lamp? He whirled about to look at the door. The chair was still as he placed it, firmly lodged under the knob.

Swiveling slowly back, he saw something which startled him even more. His clothing, dried and pressed, were carefully laid on the bed, and his gaze following the line of his trousers, settled on the sight of his shoes, gleamingly polished and neatly placed on the floor. He jerked his head away, and a cool wrath enveloped his nerves.

He allowed the trailing blanket to slip from his body and started to dress. He stepped to the dresser to check his appearance. There on the top lay Jacques' silver back brush and comb. He saw that his hair was a tangled mop, that he locked somewhat pale. He saw, too, that which caused him to turn around. A small photograph of a young man. It had slipped down on the embroidered scarf of the dresser. He righted it. But soon picked it up.

"I know this face . . ." he murmured, "Where have I seen it?" He leaned the frame toward the light. "Could it be this . . . Jacques whom Madame Cecile spoke of . . . Must be?"

However if Michael had been given a longer moment to think, he might have recalled the face. But something occurred to jar his thinking. But too much had happened for him to recall the tortured young man in the flames. For it was his face in the photograph. The memory of him was storming at his subconscious. But at that moment was looking at his own haggard white face in the mirror. He grimaced painfully! He saw his own image cloud and fade before him.

Something unusual was happening in the mirror!

The shimmering glass before him grew mottled and darkened. When it soon clarified, it showed a long green passage. The passage stretched before him. A thick vapor shimmered and curled in luminous shades over the emerald ground. Then as Michael stood cold and transfixed, the smoky substance took shape.

In that shimmering hall a lovely woman walked!

She was languorous and very beautiful. She glided with her head high, shoulders erect in a deliberate gait. She appeared to be in a hurry. Late! Rushing to keep and appointment. Mist swirled bout the hem of her gown. A gown that was tight-bodiced, made of a shimmering material. Long silver streamers drifted back from her shoulders and bare arms.

When her large, brooding eyes suddenly focused upon Michael, she suddenly paled. It was as if she was surprised to see him! Startled that it was not someone else. Michael thought intuitively, could it be that her appointed rendezvous was to be with Jacques?

He felt himself correct. Yet he leaned unbelieving his own actions closer to the mirror, endeavoring to see deeper into the passage.

She kept looking directly toward Michael, rushing toward him, her hand raised and extended with fingers curved upward in a deep and meanful greeting.

Michael felt irresistibly compelled to put his own hand against the glass. Palm to palm!

But the touch and reality of the lifeless glass with its slick coldness stopped him. He sharply pulled back. There was no third or fourth dimension, no penetrating the mirror by touch—yet the woman was there, and she saw him!

Her mouth was parted as if she were speaking. Michael strained to hear her. For a moment they simply faced each other. Her graceful figure was inclined toward him. Michael felt the full impact of throbbing impulses which was sent from her to him. The next moment she flashed a smile over her shoulders, turned on her silver heels and began to walk away. His last glimpse of her image, was her dark hair, and the silver ornament that glimmered there. She had gone. Only smoke and the dark green gloom of the passage remained.

Remaining, above all, was the woman's disastrous enticement, and the mysterious desires that took control of his mind, overwhelming Michael with passion that crept within him, and took possession of his soul. He felt no man could resist her. Years, afterwards, when in solitude, against his will, the mystical image of her would return to haunt him.

When he again lifted his eyes, Michael met his own face looking back at him, drawn and bloodless.

Later when he was taking the chair from under the door knob, a sound out in the hall chilled him! It sounded like hooves.

Cloven hooves!

That ghastly, Satanic thud was just on the other side of his door!

A terrible knowledge cleared his head. Once or twice before he heard that sound, but he had mistaken it for a rider going past. Merely an innocuous, commonplace sound—but now—? Michael could feel his heart pound; and life deflate and sicken within him. He weakened, but sudden courage returned to his heart, which at once strengthened and angered him. This latest attack upon his emotions, just enflamed him. He snatched open the door.

It was then, that the thudding hoof beats broke into a quick, light run then faded away.

Slowly with a cold tight breath burning within his chest, Michael ventured into the gloomy passage and the somber shadows. A floor-board depressed beneath his weight. It creaked. But there was nothing. Not a sound.

# CHAPTER EIGHT

"**N**o, no," Michael disputed with himself. "No." He further discredited as he meandered deeper into the dark. "It can't be that. It is not that. You are just allowing your imagination to go wild. It is too extraordinary," he said in final disbelief.

And, nearly jumped out of his skin when a sudden draft from nowhere, slammed the half-opened door, bringing him to a stop, plunging him into blinding darkness.

"That was stupid. I should have blocked the door." He slowly turned around, trying to adjust his vision. He longed to find his way beck to the room, and in another mood he hoped that he was facing the direction of the stairs. He couldn't help but think: "Whomever was trying the door . . . Certainly they did not expect to find me in the room?" He suffered a slight shiver: "Or, whatever that was! And . . . the woman in the mirror? She was hurrying to keep an appointment. Was it to meat the entity that wanted entry into the room."

Michael sighed. He warned himself to relax. He stubbornly moved forward, but with caution. For in the face of his manly courage, he suffered the grim feeling that <u>something</u> could, or might be lurking ahead in the inky void. His mind kept repeating to him so insidiously: <u>Hooves</u> "I heard them!" he spoke aloud to himself. "How Godless! Lord . . . What goes on here?" He was perspiring. His forehead and palms felt hot, but when he wiped his brow, both were clammy-cold. "It is just damn shock," he murmured feeling that he was well diagnosed his condition.

Nevertheless, he resolutely walked onward, groping with one hand outstretched, using the wall as a guide. But gradually the wall began to slope away; it rounded into another direction.

Soon, to his amazement he began to feel the slow movement of a breeze. It came wafting-up as if from a great depth, and he halted instantly, throwing his weight back, knowing that there was open space before him into which he might go crashing down!

Then something soft brushed against the bottom of his trousers-leg and there was a hissing noise directly in front of him. Of course, Michael quickly suspected just as to what it might be. However, in the face of so much strangeness, he was suspicious to really know. As he peered through the gloom, he recognized the small white outline at his feet.

"Kit—!" he cried. "What a great little creature you are." He bent over to see her: "You're probably the only rational being in this crazy house."

When Michael stooped to stroke her, the cat shot past him. Having missed her, this caused his hand to drop to the floor. His fingers found the rotting carpeting. Searching a little more he found what he thought to have been the ending of the carpet. After that was space. It was simply too dark for him to see, but his probing fingers did come in touch with the base board and the quarter-round molding there.

"Ah! This is the end of—of—something," he cried in the blinding darkness. But in reality he merely sensed a cool emptiness. A drop-off. "The stairwell. I found it. Gee, without you, Kit, I would have broken my neck . . . Kit . . . ?"

Michael reasoned that he was crouching over the edge of something uncertain. It was then that a soft light began to come out of the darkness and slowly creep over his shoulder. He twisted about to look backwards.

There, at the far end of the passage was the drifting Mimoutte, and her perpetual, wavering lamp within her hand. She came toward Michael, her flaring lamp held high to one side; and the shine of it unpleasantly emphasizing her yellow, ferret-like profile. As she drew nearer, elongated splints of light outlined Michael's low, crouching position.

Mimoutte shot him a scathing look, but his startled blue eyes biased right back at her. She caused him to feel a bit foolish being found like that. As the lamp light moved nearer, he began to look around him. Only to be caught by a terrible bewilderment that he had been crouching over an inexplicably seething blackness. He felt the great opening of the black hole, gaping just at the tip of his toes! When he began to rise to his feet, he saw a chip of broken plaster. Drawing up to his lull height, Michael looked over and then dropped the piece of plaster into the seething blackness before him.

He simply waited, feeling Mimoutte's disapproval, feeling her drawing closer to his side. After an interminable minute he heard a sound as it reached the surprising depth. It clinked. It splashed. Below him was water! When the chip of plaster reached the blackness, it caused a bright green splash! Turning green, and more green, having a luminous lighter green to its color. Surely no simple stairwell, he thought excitedly, but an un-barricaded pit!

Mimoutte stood beside him. Michael reached for her wrist. He roughly pulled her and her lamp nearer to the edge. The lamplight outline the huge black hole before them, Michael trembled as anger hissed through his nostrils. He felt like hurling the woman down into the black, gaping hole! A second later he controlled his fury and released her wrist.

Her stone-like features twisted into a yellow snarl: "Coquin!²" she hissed at Michael under narrow stormy brows. She looked at him with contempt then spat into the black hole.

"I did say, you are too kind," replied Michael. He stared down at her, feeling that the height of him gave sufficient fright to her insolence.

She lowered her eyes. Her voice, dripping with sweet acid, said: "Madame Cecile is waiting." She acted as if no incident had occurred. She played the loyal, good servant. "I, light you down, M'sieur."

Michael observed that there seemed no end to the many routes in the house. It took dimension at will. For, Mimoutte began to take him through another side-passage. However, before he allowed her to go much further, he once again took her wrist. He forced her to turn the lamp downward so its glow would light the floor ahead. It was getting so, that he did not know what he had expected to find next; he thought: Maybe evidence of hoof-marks. All he saw was dusty, threadbare carpet.

"You, too, are coquin," declared Michael showing her he understood her Gumbo.

---

² Cajun-French dirty smart-aleck

Bitterly annoyed, Mimoutte bit her lip. She shook-off his hand; she righted her lamp, at the same time her head. She drew-in a breath; lead the way before him.

The way down was totally unfamiliar to Michael, not at all the way he had come with her to Jacques' room. He was uneasy and more distrustful than ever—he questioned again his curiosity which launched him into this perilous house.

At length, they came to the wide formal staircase, the lamplight flickered in the draft; casting enormous shadows upon the dank wall, humpback and wraith-like.

Suddenly, Mimoutte halted for a second before him. It seemed to Michael that she had stopped to wait or listen or something. Her shoulders gave a little jerk; she emitted a surprising gasp, then continued to flounce downward. Michael held fast to his notion that he had no feet, but merely floated. She lifted her lamp a bit higher, and with it, her shadow altered. Verily, she seemed nothing more than a mass of cloth, bunched-in clumbily at the waist. He saw the sharp points of her bird-like elbows. Her bony profile; and her nose a beak against the wall. "Wispy of wiry hair escaped from beneath her tignon, while the tips of it cast the exotic shadow of a plumed crest.

Once on the ground floor, passing through the somber wood-paneled hall, Michael heard the rusty striking of a clock sounding from one of the velvet-hung doorways. Realizing, that he had no Idea what time it was, Michael started counting the strokes, and had just finished when Mimoutte put up her hand. She paused, her fingers crooked and with her white long nails to her lips, she slowly faced Michael. Her mind was gone; she looked lost and remote; unnatural. Her almond eyes were ablaze, while her thin mouth curved salaciously as if she had tasted a sweet morsel of forbidden pleasure.

"Midnight, M'sieur!" she announced with triumph.

"Yeah," Michael responded irritably. "Top of the clock . . . And . . . I suppose, too, the witching hour!"

Mimoutte merely stood, yellow and waxen, her lamp flaring; the burning wick smoldering, creating a sickly scent. A ribbon of smoke drifted upward.

Michael raised his eyebrows. He backed up a little. The look of her turned him cold. The woman, he realized, was submerged in a world of evil ecstasy.

"Yes." He whispered to himself, his heart quickening. "She floats!" He observed that she seemed to be listening—waiting. "For what?" he questioned. He stepped back a bit more. He fearfully studied her. Michael wondered if his chance remark held more truth than sarcasm?

"The Witching-hour," he hissed under his breath. "Maybe that is what explains the depraved atmosphere of this house?"

Mimoutte began to breath more deeply. It was if her mind; her spirit was swiftly returning from wherever it had visited in that interval.

"Heem." She uttered softly, dragging out the word in a long note until she was breathless. Then her yellow face lighted as she slowly swallowed, salivating in unholy expectancy, a black host.

Mimoutte shivered.

Michael himself could not help but shake a bit. He turned deadly serious; he stood as still as Mimoutte had. The storm was in full rage; he heard the trees moaning in the wind, as if howling in welcoming fury, a fanfare to an honored-entity. For with the last brassy twang of the clock, a terror-ridden certainty reached out to lay its grim knowledge upon Michael's heart. It was like entering a subterranean vault wherein penetrating dankness seeps into the bone, Michael knew that something ominous had entered Fournier House.

# CHAPTER NINE

The mere thought that an enigmatic presence had entered the house, perplexed all that was logic. That it had crept into the house, and not by conventional portals, held Michael frozen in its spell. He admonished himself to hold fast to all that was sound. The intuitive knowledge that it was supernatural sickened him. A sudden dizziness left him spinning. He felt as if the very passage, the walls and the floor beneath his feet began to waver. But one glance at Mimoutte told him, he was right.

Infamy lighted her uncanny being.

As he was struggling for a fresh breath and trying to clear his head, trying to overcome the suffocating fames of the kerosene, escaping from the greatly tilted lamp, he heard Mimoutte scold:

"Why you stop—you! Madame—wait."

Her remark struck him a the very essence of irony. Michael stepped right up to her, towering her being. She cowered fearing he'd sweep her aside with one stroke. The fire in his blue eyes subjugated her. She whimpered, she lifted her hem and walked ahead.

As once before the took him to a heavily curtained archway. She thrust it aside the folds of mulberry velvet for Michael to enter the book lined room. He ducked under the low hanging valance, and at last, found himself face to face with Madame Cecile.

How quaint sue looked. She seemed like a painting seated in an oval-backed upholstered chair. She was sewing and as she drew up her needle and thread, her large eyes rose to meet Michael's.

Madame rested her embroidery in her lap and studied him as he stood there, tall and handsome and a little pale under the swag of the mulberry velvet. The lamplight behind him framed his lean figure and brightened his hair.

In the interval of their long silent pause, Michael looked about the book lined walls. A log was burning evenly in the enormous fireplace. But it no longer surprised him that the andirons were fashioned like toads, or that another great golden one sat slumbering on the mantle. However the black candles sentineling this toad went unlighted.

Madame Cecile locked past him to Mimoutte, dismissing her with a hard glance. Michael felt the draperies fall close behind him as Madame's aged hand indicated the chair opposite a small table holding a tea set and a decanter of liquor.

"Sit, young man," she said softly. "No harm will come to you. Michael's young face looked relieved. A soft laugh warbled in his throat, rippling his Adam's-apple. He pulled at the creases of his trousers, then sank into the soft depth of the big chair.

"Fournier House is not without its surprises, if I may say, Madame."

"Good to see you, my young friend," greeted Madame. "I could not allow you to stay in those wet clothing."

"Good to see you. If you know what I mean."

"Oui."

"You know, among other happenings," said Michael, "I what a strange feeling came over me just before I entered this room. I experience the craziest notion that something—I don't know what,—I just can't tell you—I felt that something had entered the house. That it had merely seeped-in or that it had come-up—" Michael's shoulders sagged. "I don't even know what I am trying to say," he concluded. "Do you?"

Madame lowered her eyes. She gathered her embroidery from her lap and began thrusting her needle through the shirt pocket, finishing the cross. Michael felt it was the very shirt he had examined.

"As for myself and my nephew, dear Jacques, I offer my deepest regret for any thing you may have suffered." She raised her great dark eyes and looked into Michael's face. "Imagine what poor Jacques must suffer?" Her voice trailed away as she pulled at a tiny French-knot then broke her thread. A sleeve laid limp cross her lap. She gave it a long caressing stroke.

Although, Madame Cecile looked very, very old to Michael, her complexion bore evidence of extreme good care. Creoles of Madame's time wore veils when outdoors at all times. The sun, and its tanning rays was not valued. Indeed no! A sun tan might start ghastly rumors of cafe au lait in one's ancestry. Such could not be tolerated in the old aristocracy of New Orleans.

Madame's hair was piled in luxuriant waves, silvery-white, setting off her large, beautifully shaped brown eyes. She had a way of looking so intently at one as she spoke, that she seemed to will one to lean forward to share her secrets.

She was wearing a simply long gray dress with lace at the throat and cuffs. Also at her throat was a cameo broach made of ivory and gold. Her blue veined hands and slender fingers worked deftly at her embroidery.

Michael waited until she was ready to speak, although his curiosity made it difficult.

At last, she put aside her embroidery again and said softly, "Your coming to Fournier House is not mere chance. You have come to help me, Michael . . . particularly Jacques."

"Help?" Michael was more and more amazed. "What do you mean help . . . And, Jacques is . . . ?"

"My grand-nephew."

"He is not well?"

"Some might make that observation but, of course, a doctor would know differently . . ." Madame paused; she shifted her glance then hesitated. She was taken by a moment of helplessness. She seemed too frightened to speak further. Great fear showed in her face.

The wailing of the storm had subsided. Even the room seemed to lapse into a brooding quietness. The fire, itself, burned without a sound. Michael found himself growing tense once again. He suffered that feeling again as if another presence had come into the room. Listening . . . Waiting for whatever next Madame might have to say. It was the same kind of sensation he suffered when the clock chimed the hour there in the gloom of the hall.

Something was in the house!

Madame Cecile looked as if she wanted to break down and weep, but she restrained herself. Then she lifted the shirt to her bosom and held it to her in a light embrace.

Michael wanted to reach a hand to her in sympathy but thought better of it. After all, was she sincere, or was she acting a role?

He thought back to their talk through the curtain, still wondering by what means she had left the room. However, still in his heart he sensed an aura of goodness about her. He pressed back into the chair. He would have to wait and see.

Madame merely sat before him, her mind had drifted away into the deepest of thoughts. Michael recalled that Mimoutte's eyes were glassy and vacant. However, Madame's eyes were moist, filled with anguish over sorrowful problems.

Michael was certain, that a matter of grave significance was taking place in that shadowy, storm-lashed house. And, he had the feeling that Madame was powerless to prevent it. The hushed silence into which the old lady had fallen into affected him. Turning his eyes to the mantel, he reassured himself that the toad was as inanimate as any other decorative object. Finally he thought he could no longer cake the tension of her silence. He reached over and pressed Madame Cecile's arm.

His voice was sharp. "Madame!"

She blinked, move a little stiffly the way old people do when they have nodded-off. With a slight shake of her head she looked at Michael as if nothing had occurred.

"Why do you do that, Madame?"

She drew back startled, "Do . . . what?"

Michael surprised himself. He asked at point-blank, "I mean, why do you embroider that cross over the toad? Indeed, why the toad emblem at all?"

The curiously quiet interval had passed.

"It helps . . ." she answered, her voice trailing off.

"What does Madame mean?"

Once again she lifted her great brown eyes; a heavy breath filled her breast. "Have you ever known of anyone suffering the dark knight of the soul?" She read the blank expression on Michael's face. "No, I don't suppose you do," she went on in a soft sadden tone: "But to answer your question . . . I do this for Jacques. It helps a little . . . I think. But to do angers Camille. I know it does. She has told me that I am a stupid, senile Penelope for doing this. I cannot stop her power. But what is an old lady to do?"

She had won Michael's sympathy, but all he could say; "I do not understand. Everything here—well, I don't know what to say—"

"And, I want so desperately to tell you, I want to explain. But first, have something to refresh you. "She turned to a small table at her side. She lifted a serviette and uncovered a tea-pot and cups.

An elusive but melancholy smile touched the corners of Madame's mouth. Michael studied the gracefulness in the bend of her elbow, the fine material covering her slender arm, the old lace at her wrist. Madame's decorum, and the manner in which she poured the tea, all of the airs of an aristocratic past, revealed her background.

For a long moment, Michael studied her. She was, indeed, a lady of grace. And his thoughts took him backwards into time. He saw Madame as a girl, living perhaps in one of the great mansions along the Rue Ursulines, that street of graceful homes built with Creole wealth. He imagined her within the seclusion of a high-walled garden, exotic leaves in great iron-pots. Roses and trailing bougainvillea, the worn flagged patio where this girl of quality would sequester herself behind jasmine leaves, where a man-servant would bring something refreshing to drink, an iron fountain cascading silvery water into a stone basin of floating hyacinths.

A drink to cool the brow, the fountain serving to cool the senses.

Michael's thoughts returned to the present as Madame reached across the tray to pour a second cup of tea. Unfortunately the lamp caught her face in a most unflattering light. Michael was appalled to see how really ancient she was.

His Aunt Ernestine's Cajun-French came back, to him: 'Creoles pas mourri, li desseche.' The English translation sounded in his head as he looked closer. "Creoles don't die, they dry up." Michael pressed back in his chair wondering as to what terrible events brought Madame to the gloom and drab of Fournier House?

"No. No tea for me," he said, "thank you."

"There is a bottle of excellent old brandy," she answered, "Help yourself. A man, naturally, likes a man's drink. However, my grandmother use to tell us that, after dusk, one should sip tea and wear garnets. That dispels evil … Such we were told in those bygone genteel days. "She lifted her thin hand. Beneath the little overhang of lace, she fingered a collar of oval-cut garnets. There was a flash of royal-purple.

"Then," said Michael laughing, "What am I to do? I don't like tea, and I don't wear garnets."

He poured a drink; his great hands cupped the big brandy-glass; he sniffed the magnificent aroma.

Madame continued: "You still have nothing to fear—not really." She turned her head warily, gave a searching glance about the room as if to reassure herself that everything was all right. She touched her hand to Michael's, indicating the ring on his finger. "Because of that!" she said.

Michael looked down at the gold-set stone. Its depths of shimmering green, its flashes of yellow, the center a tiny pool of blackness—winked at him. He had worn it for so many years that he had completely forgotten the ring was on his finger.

"It was my grandfather's," he answered thoughtfully, his eyes bright with remembrance.

"I know that," she said dryly. "It is a cat's-eye."

"But of what power has a mere stone?"

"We must not scoff, young mister," she said sharply with that uncanny ability of hers to perceive another's thoughts. "I warn you! These stones have more potentiality than you can possibly believe. I know." Her fingers reached into the cuff of her long sleeve and withdrew an exact duplicate of the stone on Michael's finger. She announced: "This is the mate to that one!"

When Madame Cecile place the stone in Michael's hand, it seemed comparatively small in the square of his big palm. It was equally as beautiful as his own stone, yet this one was entirely different. Rather than sending out brilliance, it caught beams of light from the fire lamp and absorbed them.

The stone began to take on a baleful life and heat of its own. Michael handed it back to Madame.

"No, please—I want you to have it," she begged him, pushing away his hand and closing his fingers on the stone. "Take it! Take it for Jacques sake. When I am gone you will know what to do."

Michael slumped deeper into the chair, pressing his back against the big cushion. His eyes darkened. Madame's firm grip was too much, she would not release his hand. Her delicate eyebrows had become straight and implacable—will had replaced her gentleness. Her intensity, as she leaned so close to him, made Michael feel, not only that she knew his very thought, but she was forcing him to her purpose.

Michael squared his shoulders then in a sudden squall of determination, he gathered together his very own purpose and strength. He caught Madam's hand and in defiance to the resistance of her fingers, he opened them and placed the cat's-eye into her hand.

"Look! You must not think me ungrateful," he cried sternly. After all—I came to your house. I thank you for your hospitality . . ." He released a deep breath. "I sympathize with your worry over your nephew. But I don't think you are going shout this thing in the right way, I would be happy to help if I could. But whatever are you trying to say?" he almost shouted. "From the moment I set foot into this—this—!" A scalding anathema dripped acid in his throat. He bit back the mad, descriptive words he wanted to use. "What in the name of God! What th—! What's going on in this house, Madame!"

For a moment it looked as if Madame had wilted—that she would collapse into a silky heap of black taffeta and lace. The circle of tiny garnets at her throat flashed rose-purple.

"I am not psychopathic! And as a rule, I do not suffer hallucinations." He shot a finger at her. "I heard hoof-beats outside that-that room up there! Was that Jacques room?" He pointed his finger again at her; he bent over and looked her in the face.

"Come to think of it—!" Michael's thought went flying; his eyes were swimming. He seemed to be talking more to himself. "I heard hooves that afternoon it rained . . . Yes . . . Hooves! Beating around my own place. I thought it a rider . . ."

When Michael returned from his remote thoughts, he found himself biting the tip of his finger. His gaze burned through the startled face woman seated before him. He simply stared at her and waited for a straight explanation.

For a long moment she did not answer, finally she said in a dry voice: "You are thinking of leaving . . ."

Madame Cecile expressed herself very softly; and she expressed it very matter-of-factly, however, something in the way she spoke, suggested a threat. Such demeanor caused Michael to see her in a different dimension—Cecile was not so gentle—not so faint a lady as he had first supposed. He realized, too, that although he still felt she meant him no direct harm, she nevertheless would give him no rational help. Not the way he wanted. She was simply too obsessed in serving this Jacques in her way.

"When I get ready to leave," he growled curtly, "I will simply get up and walk out. Who—or, rather: What! What can really stop me?"

"Young man, you have not lived long enough to understand that what you have asked." Her ancient face was all wisdom now. Nothing beautiful remained. "Never think for a moment that we are alone—That we are actually alone! We are more spirit than flesh. And after flesh—we are spirit again! There are forces. Evil forces that can possess one."

A feeling that was bewildering and cold crept over Michael's heart. That which she stated, sent his thoughts into various paths of speculation. He thought of that evening at Rachael's, Lulu had talked strongly on that same subject. He could not help but remember, that the daily sacrifice of the Holy Roman Catholic Mass sold awfully! superbly! And mystically of the s p i r i t.

"But Oh!" groaned Michael from the depths of his private thinking, "—but that is Holy!" He did not know that he spoke his thoughts aloud until he sensed the woman's eyes upon him. She was bitterly scrutinizing his being. A vapid expression upon her face. "Yes, holy," he said looking back at her, "but what you suggest is evil!"

"Curiosity brings one to evil sometimes."

"True," he replied. "Curiosity lured me here. It was that illusive light that I noticed from my home that so whetted my imagination. You see, I had to find out what it was. To me, it was like leaving the last page of a book, unread."

"Then you are welcome to read all you wish," she said. "You have every right."

"I think I have, too!"

"But the punishment of the skeptic is that he will not believe."

"Believe, or not . . . I am willing to listen. Maybe yon and I can reach some goal help your Jacques."

"Then you will let we have my way?"

He met her eyes directly, and with a pinched mouth gave a nod of his head.

"I told you, your coming here was not mere chance."

"So you did."

Madame braced herself fixity in her chair. Her face told him that she was preparing to reveal some terrible knowledge to him. She had trouble breathing and looked painfully burdened with memories. Michael could not help but wonder as to what horrors had tormented her down the years.

She fumbled with her tea-cup, then lifted her large compelling eyes.

"You have been willed here," she said sternly. "By me, a desperate old lady. Call it, vibration, Call it a telepathic command. Anything you like. But I knew you would come. I knew it! And the only way to draw you here—that you should see that light coming from Fournier House.

For a passing second her mind seemed so remote, much like the way Mimoutte seemed to Michael, and she too, had that curious illumination in her eyes.

"Yes," she went on reflectively, and once again she caught Michael's hands. "I knew you would find your way here—And this night in particular! "The word rasped in her throat, like a key in a rusty lock. "You know what I mean, don't you?" She pulled on his hands. She faced him squarely: "What night is this, sir?"

Michael pulled his hands from her grasp. His flesh crawled; because of contact with her flesh he suffered the most unusual feeling. Once before, when he brushed against. Mimoutte, did he experience that strange feeling. So dry and unnatural.

"I don't know," said Michael. "I think it is the last of April—so what?"

"Still the skeptic!" Her eyes became mere slits in her face that reflected the lamp's fire. "And you! The possessor of the all powerful cat's eyes! And, you do not know the significance of this night . . ." Her face which as a rule was so delicately white, was suddenly flushed.

Michael himself grew flushed. He felt the heat of the fireplace pressing in on him. He turned to see it; flames began to leap higher and the legs therein the grate began to crackle as if disturbed.

Strange he hadn't noticed how unusually large and how deeply recessed the chimney-piece.

Madame called his thoughts back from the flames.

"This night," the instructed Michael firmly, "is what mortals call: Walpurgis Night."

Her great information held no news, nor meaning for Michael. His blank expression angered Madame. However, the shock of her next statement, turned him pale. For that which she intimated told the full evil of Fournier House!

In a colorless monotone, she asked:

"Do you know what we are here?"

# CHAPTER TEN

"**D**evil Cult!"
But Michael could not say it aloud. He was too deep in deep in thought to speak. When he touched his hand to his forehead his brow was hot, but his fingertips were as ice.

He thought of that moment in the passage when the clock struck midnight. He recalled it was then that he felt certain that something had crept into the house. Whatever it was seeped through, figuratively clutching and possessing everything like a noxious miasma.

Mimoutte's face came into his memory. How her face glowed. She had become catatonic. She seemed a spell of yellow ecstasy, shining in the lamplight.

When next he lifted his eyes, thinking that he had somewhat come back to his senses, he realized that the old woman sat silently opposite, holding him fixedly in her gaze. His mind was spinning. He felt the-world had tilted.

The subject before him was simply unbelievable. No sane man in a normal world could give it thought. However, from the outset, in his soul he has suspected that such grotesque madness existed in that house. He struggled to suppress it; put it aside. He almost said aloud: I can t comprehend anyone believing in such—much less worship such evil!

He felt that he had stumbled into a hollow; that he would never free himself from the terror therein. Something began pounding within himself; he realized it was his blood throbbing in his ears.

"Walpurgis Night," Madame Cecile uttered in a dry, but in a superior voice. She saw that she had devastated Michael. She saw that his soul struggled against all she intimated. "This night is called the Witches' Sabbath . . . When those who are possessed . . . Strange people. Women . . . witches such as Camille revel with Satan on such a night."

Michael spat out his opinion: "But that is myth!"

"Myth—? Myth!"

Her angry, compelling eyes subjugated him. At that same moment, too, the flames in the fireplace began to grow suddenly wild, crackling as if wishing to speak, reaching higher and higher as if wanting to break from its confine. A blast of wind tore at the house and shutters. It came cup in a mad rush, then stopped as if it wished to listen what was being said. A moment of silence passed, then the wind began to blow up again. It howled like a pack of wolves who had found prey.

"What have you to do with all this," Michael asked huskily. "Why involve me?"

"Hush!" Madame Cecile rasped, I want to tell you of the two cat's eyes. And, above all, I must tell you about Jacques . . . And . . ." Madame stopped. She cautiously looked around. She seemed very apprehensive, "and about her—Camille Fournier!"

Michael looked around; his eyes searched the room to see whatever it could be that so filled the old woman with fear. Except for the dark and antique properties, he could see nothing to warrant such secrecy.

Madame lifted her teacup. Michael observed that there was no tea within it, and suspected that there was none all along. He question why she should pretend such an act?

Then once again in her dry voice, Madame went on, she spoke reflectively of times and things past.

"A long, long time ago, before you or Jacques were born, some archeologist were searching in the Yucatan Peninsula . . . Guatemala . . . West Honduras. I don't know where exactly . . . probing the ruins of a pre-Colombian civilization. They chanced upon the tomb of a Mayan king. That tomb, whether it was for greed of knowledge, or greed for gold, was desecrated. Within that forgotten tomb rested one of the seven sacred idols of the Mayan culture, a huge stone cat. Its eyes were fashioned of precious gems, and within the jewels they ingeniously set the eyes of a real cat. One eye was intended to induce good—wonderful benevolent ages. The other to bring forth all that is evil. You must understand that this Mayan king had been blind. This cat was to lend the use of its eyes, so that recognizing both good and evil, the king might find the river to the future; that he may cross it to the sphere of everlasting life."

It seemed only natural that Michael should look down upon his ring. He lifted his hand, spreading his fingers; he saw nothing wrong in the innocuous gleam of the cat's eye; it was just a jewel.

The old woman went on: "The stones were taken from the cats head—consequently, down through the years the jewels were sold to various owners. Up to date, you and Jacques are their possessors."

"Are you saying that because I own one of these stones, that I have had these strange experiences! That because of it, you could will me here!"

"Yes! You must believe me. Not for a moment must you doubt. It is so important that you hear me out. Far back in time when your grandfather was a young-man; and my brother, who is Jacques's grandfather—at a different time—in different parts of the world, and on the same day, made their bid for the fabulous cat-eye-stones. How fortunate you are, young man that the benevolent eyes was acquired by your grandfather and came down to you. Imagine how fretful my brother became when he learned that he had acquired the malevolent jewel. He searched the world over hoping to find your grandfather that he may purchase it. But he never found the man he wanted. So evil fell upon him and Jacques."

Michael swayed his head. "That all may be, but I fail to see any other connection between your grand-nephew and me. We are strangers. And are we of the same time, you are not clear?"

"No, something happened in time to change that. Strangers on earth—Yes. But lets say that both your souls, like char oteers, circled the universe and then were parted before your earthly births. Yoo have not known or seen each other on this planet or lived at the same time, but slumbering within your, hearts is that pre-natal immortality which has made you both brothers in spirit. And where you succeeded and were blessed with good fortune—he fell! Now, Jacques is faced with this perdition. This utter loss of his soul—Unless?"

"Your story is incredible."

"Fournier House is incredible—yet you are here."

Michael tried to rise from his chair, but couldn't. It was much like that he suffer d in the tower room. It was if something outside of himself were in command of his body. Was it possible that it was Madame's will which was actually holding him. He turned eyes of great wonderment upon this gentle Creole lady.

"Jacques is your 'spirit-brother'," she insisted. "You can help him. You must. Your power is in the ring."

"If the ring means so much to you—If you really believe it can help Jacques, then take it. It is yours!" said Michael.

A pitiful, futile smile straggled across Madame's face. "Ahh," her shoulders sagged. "The ring cannot be given away so simple as that. It is yours until death."

"But you have your nephew's stone?"

"I am merely the sad custodian. Holding it because I love Jacques. I carry the stone to share some of his burden. He is still the owner. The curse is still on the boy. I did succeed somewhat in protecting him up til—She came into his life!"

After a hard breath, Madame seemed to whither. She looked so very tired. She rested her head against the back of her chair, and suddenly cried in agonizing despair.

"I have no power against her. Not Camille Fournier!"

# CHAPTER ELEVEN

Madame resumed her needlework. She searched the garment for the place she stopped her needle.

"It was high summer," Madame began to relate as she plied her silken thread and need to the shirt in her lap. "I decided on a party to celebrate Jacques' thirty-second birthday. He had stopped seeing his old friends. He had grown moody—irritable. I did not know just what was troubling him. But then, I did not know Jacques was seeing her! I planned to renew Jacques' interest in his friends. The young people he liked. His old school crowd who use to tear our family patio to bits with their fun. Silly games. I so wanted to bring back laughter into Jacques dark, handsome face.

Madame's brown eyes glistened with tears for past joy and ruined hope as her thoughts went back:

"The night was so fragrant, so balmy. The patio fountains were splashing, the night air was laced with the sweet scent of night jasmine, drifting with great white clouds and stars. You'd have thoughts artist had painted it! It is hard to remember we had such times as that. Then into that perfect night, came

Camilla. She came, bringing her own blackness, to shatter and destroy our happiness—And to totally possess Jacques.

"She was beautiful! Oh, how she looked. I see her now: She entered like an astral-spirit who had come to portend death. Marvelously dressed, her entrance caused a stir. Every lady there could only gape at such attire. Such envy. She was completely unknown to our young guest. But like an actress, Candle glided merrily upon each high strain of the violins, nodding here—there! No one knew from where she came—who invite her, or how she entered.

"She was just there! I was looking after things—Seeing everything was all right—Being, myself, a fashion-plate—when I saw her! The breath went out of me. I thought Camille was dead—Or, at the least a very, very old woman. She was a legend when I was a girl. I am certain that everyone of my generation thought her to be dead. But there she stood. Immediately, I recognized her. Aloof, unassailable in her youth, and as lovely as I had always heard."

Madame paused for a long moment. She was in the past, and Michael patiently waited for her return.

"Jacques, sleek and handsome, in the full bloom of his manhood saw her enter and flew past me like a wind. I went after him! I caught hold of his wrist as a wild woman might. I suppose he thought his old great-aunt has suddenly gone crazy. I didn't care what he thought. I said, 'Jacques, give me your ring!'"

"'But, Tante Cecile,' he replied with those great, pleading dark eyes. 'Tante, she is—She's my—my friend.'"

"I moaned in terror: Oh, Jacques, how innocently foolish. This woman's is Satan's bride. Go back, go back to your good friends. 'I think I would have done anything to get him away from her presence. He handed me his ring, but his look was of simple amazement. He, of course, did not understand my desperation; nor did he know anything of Camilla's history as I did."

"Did he know of the ring?"

"No. I never spoke of the cat s eye. Like everyone, I myself supposed it to be a myth. But in that moment, the legend of the stone of which my brother had told me was now confirmed. Instinctively I knew Camille s purpose for being there. I wanted to confront her—Slap the jewel into her hand, end send her back into from whatever darkness she had come. But at that time I did not know she had met the boy before. That there had been many meetings. How was I to know she was the cause for his black moods. That so soon she had begun to claim his soul.

"Jacques pulled away from me. Camille was standing triumphantly amid a cluster of admiring guest. I looked on as Jacques raced toward her. Their eyes met. How fatal! He was entranced like some woodland creature who has encountered his like. I saw something awaken in Jacques. It frightened me to see it. I saw evil in their silent communication. It was absolutely primitive. Jack was doomed. I saw that!"

The realization of her words caused her to close her eyes. She clasped her bands over them. She recovered herself and continued:

"Fear so enveloped my heart that I found I had no voice to speak to the boy. He saw my struggle, my desperation. His eyes looked directly through me. He was remote; impersonal as a stranger. I felt my heart pound. I felt the beating of it would suffocate me. The music, the bright voices about me became a throbbing din.

"I did not faint—I know that, I felt the room begin to spin, my knees weaken. Someone's arm upheld me. Then I found myself seated in a stiff-back chair—And, just when I opened my eyes, I saw Camille take Jacques arm. I knew they were not merely going off on a sweetheart's stroll. They moved off together, and I knew that there was a strange finality to their mission. Their goal was, as I learned later was to be wedded before Satan's altar."

Madame passed again. All life seemed to have escaped her.

Michael's legs felt cramped. His knees were too near the little table between them. He longed to rise from his chair. To get some fresh air. Madame's story had taken away his voice. He cleared his throat to speak, but she resumed:

"After that night, I saw neither of them for years, and I heard nothing from Jacques. I made inquiries. I searched. Never could I find their whereabouts. Then in time I soon realized that Jacques must have been completely in Camilla's power.

"Then one morning my dear servant was shopping in the French Market and through conversation with another servant. He brought a story to me that a carriage had taken supplies to this house—Camille Fournier's ancestral home. Such knowledge brought new life to me. Vengeance as well! I made up my mind to find them. I sought out this house and forced my way in! I came here to fight and rescue my nephew. I've bean here ever since. I feel my task is nearing its end, now. That is why I depend upon you for help. The crisis is near!"

Michael suddenly rose to his feet. He bumped his knee against the table and almost over turned it. He had sat in that chair too long. He felt he had hear too much.

Madame Cecile said: "Need I warn you that you, too, are in grave danger—In spite of your ring! Camille survives on the youth of men! She knows of you—Yes she does!"

Michael frowned. This was the crowning fantasy to the mysterious tale he had been listening to.

"What in the world are you talking about, lady!" Michael cried sharply. "How crazy is all of this! Such can not exist. What do you mean survive? This woman survives upon the youth of men—What! He screamed. "On flesh? Blood? Is Jacques—? Oh my God! Am I a blood sacrifice? Lady, I can't believe what you are telling me. Or what in God's name am I saying!"

Suddenly Madame was standing beside him. Michael parted his lips to protest, but the old woman quickly placed her fingers over his mouth.

"Silence," she whispered in frightful awareness. "I knew that people from your world cannot understand such things. How well I know. But you are on the threshold of hell."

Again she motioned for silence and pointed to the curtain masking the archway. Michael saw the curtain waver. He understood that someone was on the other side.

With her small hands, Madame pushed Michael across the room, and backed him into the deep recess fronted by the octagonal windows. Quickly, frantically, she pulled the cord which drew the draperies closed to hide him.

"They are coming!" she whispered, "Jacques and Camille! They must never find you!"

Michael told her as he peeped through the parting of the curtains. "But Mimoutte knows I am here."

"Mimoutte!" That creature!" Madame rasped. "She is nothing. Besides, she is afraid of me and dare not to disobey. You will find things out about Mimoutte."

Michael thought wryly that he had already surmised a good deal about that loathsome woman.

Madame urgently murmured a last command: "Remember what I have said. I count on you to save Jacques. When time comes you will know what to do!"

With a final stern look she firmly closed the small opening in the draperies through which Michael was peering. The last he saw of Madame was the white of her slender hand. But he found himself consumed with curiosity about Jacques and especially, he admitted to himself, Camille. He wanted to see and to talk with them. Why had he allowed Madame to put him behind the draperies?

"What a macabre little house?" Michael thought to himself. He felt like a boy playing hide-and-go-seek within the heavy folds of the musty velvet.

Soft flashed of lightning glimmered behind the lace curtains as rain tapped insistently upon the windowpanes. Michael held his breath to listen and to spy through the narrow slit in the velvet. Thunder rolled softly in the distance.

# CHAPTER TWELVE

Madame Cecile preservingly poked at the smoldering logs with the enormous recess of the fireplace. It took a while to start up the flames for dampness had fallen down the flu and once or twice the flakes hissed and spit. One little flame fell out upon the hearthstone. She kicked it into the grate with the tip of her silken shoe. She fancied the burning coal looked like a face. But what she was really doing was crating a normal atmosphere for whomever was to enter. At last when she had completed her task, she returned the poker to its rack.

When once again she stood erect, she brushed back some faint hair from her forehead while the lamplight caught her in bold profile. She looked slim and straight in her long grey muslin gown. Her chin was firmly set and high; her white, blue-veined hands were folded in front of her. With her back to the fire, she faced the door. Defiance and unconcealed hatred blazed in her eyes.

A stunning, remarkably beautiful woman entered. Michael immediately recognized his lovely vision; it was she who he had seen in the mirror in the tower room. But he felt that ones before he had seen her. Was it in a dream, and wondered where else?

"So this is Camille?"

She was indomitable. Her enchantment could not be denied, her beauty was flawless. She was dressed in the very purple gown. He remember the long silver streamer that was flung across her white throat. It was so draped that it met another, and they cascaded over her shoulders like silver wings. Cowering a few steps in back of Camille entered the pitiful figure of Maltese's Cecile nephew, Jacques. How broken his spirit was he. He might have been yet a young man but all the blitheness of his years had gone from him. Michael wondered at what terrible price fed his vitality been spent. He was simply wasted. His eyes, of which his aunt spoke so lovingly, were now, nothing more than dark circles of horror.

Madame shivered at the ghastly appearance of her nephew. But she held herself strong. She felt forced to acknowledge Camille's presence. She nodded icily. Bit Madame Cecile aristocratic temper could not be contained. In a sudden fit she spat out something contemptible. Camille covered at the sudden attack. Even the elements took offense for at that second thunder broke over the house and Michael missed whatever was said.

Camille lifted her head and broke into a spell of laughter. She vainly touched the silver ornaments holding back her lustrous hair. She glance about and spied the tea table between the chairs.

"My! My! Dear, dear Tante Cecile," she cooed in a honey-smooth voice which held an underlay of venom. "Tante, dear? Have you been entertaining!"

Michael shot an excite glance at the table. True, only one tea cup sat there, but there was evidence of two glasses.

"Like you, I too, have friends," Madame returned somewhat acidly. "Maybe to your great surprise, Camille, a friend has come to help me."

"To do just what, dear Tante—Help you to embroidery things?" Camille picked up the shirt, She looked at the silken cross over the pocket, then flung the garment aside. She lifted, her eyes to the old woman in contempt.

"The cross offends you?"

Camille laughed: "Oh, Tante Cecile!" She arched her creamy shoulders while continuing her laugh of malicious, insolent, indecent amusement. She was like a snake coiled and ready. Vainly she once more touched her hand to her beautiful dark hair. The silver ornaments there, flashed like rapier blade. Finally she scoffed, "What a question?"

"I thank you not to address me such as that. It sickens me!" Madame Cecile turned away from Camille.

"Oh, dear! How sad that I should not address Jacques' favorite, like she were my own dear Tante. How cold. How so not family-like, dear Tante." Her lips drew back in a horrid grimace. Suddenly Camille stopped her biting mockery. She looked up at the mantle. "But dear!" she cried and slinked over to the enormous fireplace. "You haven't lighted our Beel!" her voice throbbed with excitement, "You haven't forgotten what night this is—Jacques knows!"

Madame lifted unwilling eyes to the mantle, and to the gleaming toad squatted there. It perched there with its mouth agape, slothful and sordid. The insatiable idol seemed to wait in idle evilness. How she hated the sight of it. She looked away.

At the mentioning of Beel's name, a ghastly cry broke from the depth of Jacques throat. He flung his hand to his face. He cowered, knowing the dreadful horror of his future. With trembling shoulders he continued to sob. Pitiful, deep chested sobs as only a man can give.

"But . . . Jacques," Camille murmured in a voice that was half rebuking and half amusedly tolerant. She postured with one hand on her hip, but her incurious eyes seemed blank with no concern for that suffering creature she had ruined. She shrugged her shoulders, then fixing an uncompassionate look upon the aunt.

Camille turned to her task. She raised her arm to the shelf. It was well above her head. The white oval of her back showed through the panel of her gown, and her rounded hips were snugly edge in by the close fit of it. The tendrils of her black hair nestled and swaggered in the nape of her neck. She made a charming picture. Standing on tip-toe she stretched her lovely body to its full height.

Suddenly a spark brightened from her fingertips. She lighted the tall candles on either side of the idol Beel. Afterwards, she touched her flaming fingers to the hollow of the toad's belly. A sweet vapor began to drift from the hollow eyes and belly of the gleaming thing. Soon a most delicious odor filled the strange and antique chamber, and Michael was privileged to spy upon it all.

Jacques was bent over his great-aunt's shoulder, trembling. Madame caressed him; stroked his head. He seemed nothing but wasted flesh and bone. The white-wheat of his manhood squandered.

"No, Jacques," she murmured as though he were a child. "We have not lost yet! Pray Jacques. Have you forgotten? 'Though your sins be scarlet, I will make you as snow . . .'"

Jacques lifted his head and looked past his aunt, but with unseeing eyes for her, but with eye a only for Camille. However, at that moment, that sinister sorceress was whispering to the monstrous symbol on the mantle—Adoring Beel in the image of a toad.

To Michael, it sounded as if she were speaking the Gumbo-incantation Mimoutte used. Ever since Jacques and Camille entered the room, something had been stirring his memory. Michael knew there was an interconnected memory of them both. He felt a kind of sympathy for Jacques, that ruined soul.

Certainly, Camille was the mystical woman in the mirror. Somehow he dimly recalled that there had been for him also, an intimate, joyous experience with this woman. Somewhere with all the confusion and the mystery of Fournier House. He knew her. A déjà vu, as it were. However at the time and place his thoughts could not bring it together very clearly. He sensed the pull of an invisible bond pulling them all together. He looked at Camille. In spite of her wickedness, Michael loved the allure of her. It reached out to take him.

An upheaval of thunder suddenly broke from the drenched-lull of the storm. Its volley trembled Fournier House to its foundation! Seizing Michael, and bringing him up from the deep well of his thought and observance.

Camille thrilled: "What fury! Wonderful! Wonderful!" she cried. Her long fingers gripped her shoulders as she embraced herself in joyous fulfillment. "For you! You! Adorable Beel—Master!" She raged in homage to the gleaming toad.

She flung her head back and laughed. "Marvelous!" she ranted between fits of laughter while the storm lashed the world. "A fanfare of fury for you, dear Beel—Angle sent!" She stopped short, her eyes gleaming. She realized the honed-malevolence of her satirical thrust, "Angle sent . . ." She lifted her pointed finger above her head and began to laugh more wild than before. She trembled, excited seeming to grow madder and madder.

Suddenly she caught hold of her fancy. She stopped. The storm stopped. Camille turned from the mantle and the golden idol above her head. She spun about in a grand sweep. It suggested the swag of a medieval cape. Her skirt swung, then settled softly around her slim ankles. Her silver slippers caught the light and flashed. The flames in back of her outlined every curve of her body, reawakening even more her seductive spell upon Michael. He watched her; he also understood even more the enchantment which had conquered Jacques will.

Madame lifted her head, her mouth an angry line. She gave a deadly glance at the woman before the fire, thinking the worst of thoughts. She held her nephew, Jacques closely to her. She spat the words: "She-Devil! Witch!"

"Stop hanging on, Cecile. You are useless—Inadequate. You bore me! You and your simpering. Your absurd embroidering. What a fool, Cecile."

The courtesy-title: "Tante or Aunt" was gone. What was courtesy to Camille but an irrelevant thing. She had come into full power. She was indeed, a she-devil, a witch in icy command. All authority was Camille's. She almost levitated. A kind of vapor drifted from her person, and ringed its illusion about her. She glowed.

Suddenly the entire chamber became illuminated by a cold, supernatural light, Camille, then became as a burning coal but a strange kind of coal that was as transparent as crystal. There was too, a sweet smelling scent of aromatic-balms. Common things in the room looked strange, taking on fantastic shapes.

Madame bravely persisted. "Terrify yourself. You haven't won yet, Camille."

"I will have my victory. In an hour—even less. You will know!"

"Not his soul! It will never be yours. Nor will it belong to Beel!" Madame began to tremble. The knuckles on her thin, clenched hands were white. In desperation she cried a final threat: "I have found the way to defeat you, Camille! I will triumph I Banish you to the hell where you belong!"

At that, Camille closed her eyes and inhaled deeply; the hiss of her breath was audible across the room. She pressed her palms together. She lifted her arms and with garbled vowels, she began to mutter words and sounds that were totally alien. She entered into a cold trance; as she uttered her malediction, she began to glow. The house trembled with thunder. The fire flared. The strength of her evil was everywhere.

When she again opened her eyes, they seemed implacable. She strode across the room to the archway. She thrust the heavy velvet aside, and held it as she waited imperiously for Jacques to follow.

Madame allowed Jacques to slip from her embrace. But she wanted so desperately to keep him. However, Jacques, himself was powerless to resist. Helpless and dub as a sleep-walker, his shoulders slumped; his spirit cowering, Jacques obediently followed his mistress.

Before exiting the chamber; before she allowed the curtain to fall back, Camille faced the old woman and stared at her for a long moment. The corners of her brightly painted mouth began to twitch. She could not restrain the smile of assurance. Her eyes told of her impending victory.

After Camille's departure, Madame Cecile staggered wearily toward her chair. Trembling, alone in her anguish, she fell into the silken depths of the great chair.

Blinking she had fainted, Michael rushed from his hiding. He reached over the back of the chair, hoping to find her wrist. However, all his searching hand discovered was the upholstery. He quickly circled the chair. He stopped. He looked there not believing his eyes. It was empty! The room was empty. He was alone!

Only Jacques shirt lay there—ripped to shreds.

# CHAPTER THIRTEEN

The corn shirt lay there with its limp sleeve outstretched toward Michael. The pearl button on the cuff winked in the wan light, seeming to entreat help for its master.

With heavy breath, Michael backed away from the chair. Some how its emptiness frightened him. In a sudden siege of temper Michael wanted to kick over the chair. But something made him stop, and he just stood there, frowning at the carpet; trying to think of a rational solution of the situation which confronted him. All at once two emotions struck at him—mystery and anger. Anger because Madame Cecile begged for assistance, and then she disappeared like that again. The mystery of so many unanswered question left behind.

Suddenly his eye caught a flicker of movement at his side. He spun around. The curtains in the archway were swaying! He charged over and savagely caught the heavy velvet and pulled them down from their hangings. A cloud of dust billowed-up, suffocating the air.

Beyond the archway, the corridor lay dark and empty. Not a sign of life stirred. Even the storm had abated. It seemed to have drifted away with the wind, to seek a place to brood and wait, leaving Michael in a hollow of silence.

He strained to see his way. His very footsteps thudded after him; he turned about to see if he were really alone. At last, he thought he recognized an object. It looked like a grandfather's clock.

"Maybe," he thought, "this way could bring him to the front entrance. He drew closer to the towering mahogany bulk against the wall.

"Oh, soy God!" Michael cried in terror. His discovery left him cold. "It is not a clock—A coffin!"

The horrid long box was propped against the wall. It was but an accident that Michael looked through the plate glass that made up its lid.

Within lay Mimoutte. Her yellow waxen face shone out at him!

A cry strangled in his throat. He rushed from the thing in disgust. A feeling of being isolated from all human warmth, made Michael want light desperately.

He went back into the room. The fire was smoldering and the lamp flickered weakly. He stepped near to Madame's chair. He saw her tea-cup.

"Yes. Your tea-cup. Little wonder why it is dry?" Michael said to the empty chair. "Ghost have no need of drink, do they, Madame. That is also the reason why I sensed so strange a touch when our hands met, Spirit! No substance. Mimoutte, too! That is how you disappear. "Michael discovered himself trembling." And . . . what of that thing? That thing in the box—A walking corpse. A reanimated th—A zombie!" He rasped. "Help you, Madame? God help me!"

Michael lifted the lamp from the table. He wanted to turn the wick higher, but in his haste, he turned the little wheel the wrong way—A wisp of smoke curled up the frosted chimney and the flame went out!

Trapped once again in sudden gloom, Michael looked toward the fireplace for light. No logs lay on the heart, so he could not refuel the fire and the candles beside Beel were out.

He thought of his experience in the tower room. We thought, supposing that grizzly thing would take on life as if had once before.

"Then," he cried, "I will smash that damn'd thing to bits! He put down the lamp and snatched one of the iron pokers from its rack. He would not suffer that bizarre consequences again. He looked up at the toad. The gleaming thing seemed to be watching, waiting!

His eyes made a quick search, hoping to find some matches to relight the lamp. His fingers were groping around the marble table top when he heard a faint sound behind him.

Michael suddenly twisted his neck and chin toward the mantle. There was a sliding. A faint grating, as if stone were being dragged over stone. He tightened his grip on the poker. He stepped to listen, but not detect the place of that creaking sound.

Just then the crimson log crumbled. Its embers flickered blue, then puffed and whispered to death in the down draft of the flue. All he could see was the black silhouettes of the iron toads.

Then the sound returned!

A light flickered in the vast recess of the fireplace. A vertical crack began to appear in the back wall of the chimney. The great stones began to tremble and slide apart. The heavy soot upon them began to slide away. The blackened bricks parted. Presently a thin line of light appeared. It glimmered in the gloom. It shimmered green.

The sound of the old stones continued to creak and move, growing wider. The widening and ominous rumble of the fissure gave Michael a fright but he would not turn away from its interest. Soon the fissure was a high as the fireplace. A shaft of tremulous green light cut its path into the darkness.

Michael shaded his eyes and tried to see beyond the light. He saw a long passage. Its green radiance lighted the path ahead and somehow seemed to intermingle with a kind of mist. He wondered if he had somehow discovered an exit from the room.

A foreboding restrained Michael, but interest lured him to follow the luminous light to its source. He reassured his grip an the poker. He spat on it, took a deep breath then ducked under the mantle, stepping over the smoking ashes.

Once in the passage he soon found himself lost within the foggy, drifting vapors.

Finally, at the far end of the passage, his head bumped into a low, stone arch. His hand patted and searched blindly the curved stone over his head. After another client's hesitation, Michael bent his long frame under the arch. He found he had to make a step downward, then another one. This place him on a shale ledge. The stratified clay, stuck out from the main wall which formed something like a small balcony. From there he saw that the balcony protruded over an enormous cave.

A couple of pieces of two-by-fours, made of rotting cypress branches served as a precarious railing. A yard or so onward, Michael came upon, a muddy staircase that had been cut into the side of the dank wall. All this lay beneath the very foundation of the old house. He leaned over and looked down, and looking up again, he realized that he was in a great hollow. A subterranean chamber!

He wondered if it was all man-made, hollow out by slave labor from the old settlement days. If so, he marveled at such a formidable task since New Orleans is below sea level. Michael wondered, too, if pirates had discovered an old bed of the bayou, enlarging it; shoring it with enormous stones to make a treasure-cache.

Michael pressed his forehead against the cool dank of the wall. He began to think about the history of the bayou.

The drifting bayous in, and surrounding New Orleans in the mid-eighteenth-century were not always peaceful. Pirates and freebooters swept the Gulf of Mexico and Caribbean, plundering Spain's gold laden galleons. Some corsairs would enter the bayous directly from the Gulf onto Delta country, but others would sail swiftly into Lake Ponchartrain and then slip quietly into the wooded bayous fringing the lake shores, including Bayou St. John.

Rene Beluche, pirate and privateer, boasted that Bayou St, John was his territory! He and his lieutenants would have known better than anyone when a bayou shifted its course and left this subterranean remains.

Could one of those 'cut-throat-lieutenants' of long ago, had in time came up to be the respected Fournier of Creole-Aristocracy, and whose, descendant, Camille, found another use for this secretive chamber!

Michael looked over the railing. It creaked at the slightest touch. As he looked down, wet warm air rose into his face. From time to time the mist would drift away, and there, below him, he saw the origin of the green light!

Water!

'The unexpected, soft, swampy lapping surprised Michael. He leaned his ear toward its sound, The marvelous inventiveness of nature had placed beneath Foamier House a subterranean bayou. He looked upon its luminous circle, then lifted his sight to follow the updraft of steamy vapors. He expected to see the roof of the cave, but all he could discern was a kind of gaping chimney. He understood that, in someway, it must have been a part of the tower.

Memory took him back to the beat of hoofs which thudded outside of his door; his blind walk in the black hall upstairs; and that strange recess which yarned inches away from his toes.

"And . . . this is what I almost fell into?" he murmured in fearful speculation.

Suddenly: Something white flashed below—

"Mimoutte!"

Shocked. Her name rasped in his throat.

Her mysterious resurgence left him frozen. He would never forget that dead, waxen face he view in her coffin. Michael could set turn his eyes away frost the metamorphosis which had come over her. She came up from her chrysalid like a diabolical moth. She was as Madame said: A creature. A revenant thing. moved about jerky and unnatural.

It was the first Michael had seen Mimoutte without her constant lamp. A flowing white vestment covered her scarecrow body. It flounced about her naked toes, and was split clear up to her armpits. Even her yellow-brown arms were bare; her hands and arms were reverently outstretched. She had removed her tignon which revealed her wild bushy hair. Hair that was brushed out eight inches from her narrow skull.

Her fingers pinched the side folds of her gown; she drew the side out to a wide arc and began to ake herself in all her white finery.

"But why white?" Michael asked as he studied this latest parody on sanctity. She appeared to be listening and hearing some rhythm within her brain. Her eyes were glassy. They biased with a madness. A moment later she began to dance about the pit which skirted the pool.

She was a priestess!

Mimoutte lifted her arms to whatever godless thing she worshiped. She stopped. She began to shake and tremble. Her golden earrings were circling fires, flashing as she threw her head and hair backwards. Suddenly she began to beat her chest in a frenzy. She chanted in high pitch cries!

Beyond the boiling surface of the pod rose three craggy steps. The uppermost step stretched out like a dais. It made a kind of plateau. In the center of which was a throne. Positioned on either side of the throne were a pair of great granite toads—from within the rarity of their bellies, and from the hollow of their eyes drifted flame and incense.

Mimoutte continued her chanting, her voice rising to a screech. Suddenly, in a fit of ecstasy, she passionately flung her body down before the dais mid throne. Her voice cried its hymn, to evil. Her words drifted up with the steaming vapors into the black hollow above.

From within the watery depths of the pool came a faint gurgling sound. Michael wrenched his eyes from. Mimoutte to the pool.

Something black had bobbed to the surface!

A cold perspiration perched upon Michael's golden eyebrows. What had Mimoutte's evil chanting called up! He stiffened and held his breath in dread anticipation of a creeping presence within his view.

Horror drugged he looked on with awe and fascination.

Little black globe, no larger than his fist were stealing out of the dark expanse of green water. They advanced out of the water, then onto the bank of the pool in small groups. Whatever it was began to hop and hop like wet hunks of mud.

"Toads!" He whispered. "Toads!" It turned Michael's stomach to watch, yet he had an irresistible urge to witness their mission. The creatures seemed to increase in size as they advanced to Mimoutte's prostrated body.

As they jumped over and about her body, Mimoutte changed positions. She got to her knees. She lifted her arms, but never once did she step her chanting. She seemed to be singing the toads up from the water's edge. Soon more and more of the hideous hopping toads slithered out of the pool, and still Mimoutte sang until the horny creatures seemed to be everywhere.

They advanced in a deliberate manner as they hopped toward a long muddy shelf. To Michael, the shelf resembled a jury-box where each toad took a separate place as if it were assigned to it. As if the toads had enacted the like many time before, seeming as it were a routine.

A sudden horrible apprehension almost swept Michael from the ledge. It biased into his mind as to what caused the toad's amphibious features to appear so forbidding and hideous. Their expression looked so human in character.—But written there upon each malevolent face of each toad, who conformed what was to be a jury, was the face like that of cruel tyrant in history!

Michael locked closer. It looked undeniably so. These toads were once the soul's of tyrants!

"My God!" Michael felt faint. He sensed himself sway amid the steaming vapors and the horrible upheaval of his thoughts. "Had Mimoutte chanted them up from hell!"

The crazed woman finally stopped her wailing. Michael welcomed the relief.

She floated up to the jury, smugly facing the grim creatures before her. Her shining eyes, simply blazed with madness. Instantly the toads hushed their cacophony. They became as rebuked children in the presence of a sub-priestess, who had taken charge. Their croaking dissonance went dead.

The white of the toad's bellies heaved and puffed from their labored breathing.

Then a sudden gurgling bubbled from the pool, disturbing the silence. Mimoutte jolted. She twisted her neck around, jutting her pointed chin over her thin shoulder. The water began to eddy more wildly, spilling over the edge of the pool. Something was thrashing up from the secret depths of the water. Finally something strange emerged!

Michael could not tell exactly what it was, there in the gloom below.

But Mimoutte knew! She was poised, transfixed, spittle oozing from her gaping mouth, and a crazed look in her eye.

Michael leaned forward for a better look. A sudden weakness swept over him. He saw what seemed like an enormous toad—Or! Was it the bent figure of a stunted man? The sight defeated him. He slumped against the wall for a rest. But when he heard the sound of a new, but very familiar voice, he sprung forward. A woman's voice cried:

"Beel!"

Unmistakably! It was the honey-smooth voice of Camille! She had been, obviously, sequestered in the shadows, quietly surveying the ceremonial rite, solemnly awaiting her sovereign-lord.

Her syllable so sweet, that she might have been calling to her lover. A second, passed; she called the name again, cooing with tenderness to her monarch.

"Beel!"

Slowly and dreamily Camille moved into the green translucence of the cave. Michael learned to his surprise that she had been stationed directly beneath the ledge upon which he stood. As she came forward she allowed a great hooded-cape, of blackest velvet, to fall from her head and shoulders.

The mystical light cut through the thin gown she wore. The hem of the gown was designed in irregular strips and tatters, which tumbled to her ankles and dainty bare feet. The cloth clinging to her was of such delicate folds that it seemed to have no substance, pressing close to her thighs and calves, revealing the outline of her form; her supple flesh; the lines of her breasts and hips.

When she lifted her curved and dimpled arms; her black hair tumbled loosely about her shoulders. She drifted more and more into the shimmering light. For all practical purposes, Camille might have been naked.

A bright note warbled sweetly in the flesh of her white throat.

"Beel!" Camilla cried. "Beloved Master!" Her lovely arms wavered in a sweeping gesture. She bowed.

Soon Mimoutte moved forward in that curious floating manner. Her hands were outstretched; over her forearms lay a long cloth of rich purple. She bowed to her mistress and waited for Camille to take the cloth.

The material was a splendid Renaissance piece of the fifteenth-century. Its thick brocade was richly needled with threads of pure silver and gold. Seed-pearls manifested a great toad in the center. The border was fixed with jewels.

While Michael had never before seen its like, its appearance, however, told of its use. It was a casket pall used to cover the dead. As Camille unfolded the pall, the more it blazed with gems; surely it had been originally intended for royalty.

Camille drifted to the edge of the pool and waited, holding the velvet open. A large head with a thick neck rose above the hem, then heavy shoulders bulged beneath the dazzling raiment. The folds of the feature took the outline of a figure. A strange, undefined shape. Human and yet not human! Swarthy hands took the edge of the cloth and tightened it to its person. It moved away from the water into the light toward the craggy steps. The figure paused, slowly turned and faced the waiting assemblage.

Beel, His Satanic Highness smiled.

# CHAPTER FOURTEEN

s Beel shook the water free from his heavy, curly head it coursed in rivulets down his face and rolled off his chest and muscular thighs like droplets of liquid fire. He was black, but not like a native. His color was the black of charred wood or seared stone. His flashing eyes in his huge glowing face were slits of vulpine cunning. His cheeks were round as if they were full of delicious secrets, tidbits to savor and swallow salaciously, one by one. His body was covered with thick curly hair. He was a man; he was an animal. Nothing of his like had walked the earth since the dawn of time.

Michael pressed his back against the wall. He felt weakened, he was cold with fear. Never could he tell this to anyone. Such a tale could only be attributed to hallucinations. The incident would haunt him always. He swallowed. He watched.

Beel tightened the mortuary cloth about his bulk. He skirted the boiling pool, then mounted the steps to his throne. He sat back. Camilla came forward and bowed before him.

The master glanced indifferently at his subject. Beel raised and lowered his heavy wolf-brows; cruelty and mockery smoldered in his yellow eyes. He threw back his trembling shoulders and laughed at her. His pointed canine teeth gleamed.

In the face of his mockery, Camille held herself proudly before him. She filled her breasts with a deep breath. She looked at Beel forcefully, concealing her own venom. She smiled and made a low sweeping bow. She had to, it was expected of her. No matter how hated her task, Camille humbled herself by placing her forehead upon the bottom step. Her beautiful hair flawed over the slimy stone.

"Highness, Highness!" she murmured entreating Beel, lifting her dark head slightly. "Great one . . . My power, wealth and youth, my voluptuous body are granted by your generosity only. You know that I have served you well. I am faithful. I am yours, dear Master!"

"Yes. We are aware of such. But get on with our business," demanded Beel drumming his fingers upon the arm of his throne. "You know that servitude and faithfulness are but obligatory in our business! Hurry! You know I have worlds of commitment before this night. Present to me your dues—Your accomplishments. What victory have you to offer me?"

"Oh, how well I can show you, Master!" Camille rose gaily to her feet. She went up another step to the throne. "Mimoutte!" she cried and clapped her hands for her hierophant to step forward. "Grow, Mimoutte . . . Impart your secret knowledge, resume your chanting. Beel must know!"

Mimoutte spread her yellow fingers and in a low, controlled vibrant voice began her chanting. Bravely she spoke strange wards to Beel. She had now become the prosecuting attorney. She represented her Mistress. Her monkey-like features glowed. From moment to moment she turned from Beel and looked toward the jury of toads.

Mimoutte looked at them. So did Camille. Then a sudden croaking approval went up. Their foolish mouths flapped in a kind of mutual accord. Then they became quiet and gaped at the ghastly rag of a woman as she continued her presentation.

It sounded as if the toads had cried the name of 'Jacques'. They grew still and waited. Mimoutte chanted, and it sounded more clear than before: 'Jacques' 'Jacques' . . .

Whatever information Mimoutte reported, pleased both Beel as well as the toads. For their croaking rose and rose until it reached a crazy frenzy, insane and hideous. A victory had apparently been won!

Michael's thoughts streaked back to the book lined room. He recalled Camille's boast: "In an hour, you will know my victory!" He drew in a burning breath and turned his gaze blow him.

Satisfaction glowed within Camille. She tightened her breath and stood before Beel, tall, proud and victorious. She had become as an ivory figurine.

A puzzling grimace came over Beel's features. He rose and looked down at the proud woman before him. The cloth which had been resting over his knee, tumbled. Its fall drew Michael's attention as his followed to see where it had fallen. He observed hooves.

Cloven-hooves!

Hooves whose thud had hunted Michael the night he looked out at the light. That wet afternoon as he closed his front door, he again hear hooves as they beat through the garden and woods.

Beel drew the extravagant cloth closer to his person. A change had gradually come over him. Like a chameleon Beel had changed the color of his skin. He changed from black to a ruby-wine. He was lighted and glowing from within like an translucent ember. Deeper and more claret became his color until he was like heated lavender. His mouth was wet with spittle. His lips were upturned in an reptilian grin. He lifted his arm, the jury of toads fell silent.

Camille went into a silent ecstasy of adoration. She grew limp with devotional idolatry. She listen, seeming to hear a satanic locution issuing from Beel, swaying now in a state of amorous enchantment.

Michael leaned forward to hear whatever Beel was shaking to Camille. But he could hear little and understood less. An oppressive silence bore down upon everything. Its stillness pressed upon, Michael seeming to smother him.

The toads were also listening; craning their necks toward Beel. Mimoutte cowered at Camille's side; her figure looked humped and frozen, while her monkey-like features were pinched and reflecting the sickly green of the light.

A matter of tremendous importance occurred below. However, whatever the incident, its great meaning escaped Michael. He knew only that all at once he suffered a staggering of evil. The power of it rose up from the steaming vapors to touch him and to lay its fearful siege upon his brain.

As far as Michael could discern, Beel was enacting some dread ritual. A spell! A metamorphosis! The circumstance of it caused a terrible and inexplicable awe to creep wearily over everything. Michael swept his astonished blue gaze about the cave. He questioned and wondered as to just what all eyes were looking upon? What could be so gravely contemplating!

A gentle freshness began to steal in from the secret recesses of the cave. Its coolness revived Michael, bringing him up from the depths of dread and bewilderment. Even the light began to filter and soften. It came in pale ivory tunes, such as the light he first encountered from his window.

It seemed as a twilight illumination such when drowsy light trails the dusk of the horizon. The light settled upon everything, sweetening the dank horror of the cave. Its golden-peach petals, rimmed with white fire danced like monstrous wings over and around Beel.

But Beel was no longer in his strange abominable form! He had returned to his once angelic glory. A fallen archangel who formerly stood with the seven before the throne of grace. And, Michael saw with his own eyes the wonder which so enchanted this strange and bizarre court.

A beautiful young man was on the dais for all to see! He was wonderful to look at in limb and body. He glowed with perfection and graces from crown to foot. Perfection and modesty lighted his face. His smooth, gold head shone in the warm light. He allowed the pall to slip to his waist where one hand upheld the cloth below his naval, revealing his high chest and the marvelous flesh tones of his naked torso. Then another kind of light seemed to shine right through him giving more grace to his extraordinary and personable beauty. His finely cut lips glowed with innocence. His frank blue eyes held all the unspotted purity of youth. Be was at once trustful.

This is no mere spirit! Thought Michael. He turned suddenly cold and trembled. He flung his hands to his eyes as though he sought to imprison this fearful and incredible experience.

Suddenly Michael knew that he must shake his head. Circulate his blood. He felt himself swaying and he feared he would blackout. He grimaced painfully then closed his eyes with a hard squeeze. His old school monsignor came to mind.

He found himself muttering: "I dread the loss of heaven and the pangs of hell—" He lifted his hand to his forehead. His brow was cold as frost.

Camille with bowed head was backing away from the dais. The sheer gown covering her began, to fade under the shadows formed by the ledge.

Every goggled eyes followed her. Mimoutte was close to the ground as low as a serpent.

Soon Camille emerged and paused aureoled in the green light. Beel had changed, too. Presiding over everything, he glowed a brassy yellow. Camille quivered with anxiety. One curved voluptuous and hung back as if she waited for someone to follow.

She stopped back into the shadows an inexorably pulled her great victory to the dais of sacrifice! A sob broke from Jacques trembling lips. Its pitiful cry of pain and remorse resounded in the dank hollowness of the cave. The cry rose then fell like a condemned creature whimpering for the loss of its own immortal soul. The light fell upon his head and gleamed over the white of the material he wore.

Michael recognized it. His garment was the shirt Madame Cecile worked on. It's tatters hung about his naked form. Jacques hesitated. He cowered back, but Camille prodded him on. She had to display Jacques—her conquest, her prize.

Jacques' face showed the full corruption which had overtaken him. His once perfect face was yellow and twisted. His nose had become hawk-like; his cheeks wasted and sagging. Awful black smudges hung under his horror-filled eyes. He had become hell's possession, a fright to behold. Camilla grinningly dragged him closer to the throne. She slowly moved in back of Jacques where her slender fingers caught the collar of his shirt. She nuzzled her mouth to the side of his neck, then slowly eased the tattered shirt from his body. Shamed and nude, Jacques' spare body was before all to view.

The jury of toads looked on with wet gaping mouth. Mimoutte curved and closer about Jacques lower form and laughed.

"Come . . . Jacques," Camille sweetly urged, soothing him through the gates of hell, "It's time."

With sickening heart, Michael looked upon the appalling deterioration which had come over the man. There was no resemblance to the handsome youth he saw in the book lined room. The tragedy of Jacques condition filled Michael with personal sympathy for him. He hated to look, but could not turn his eyes from the proceedings. From his groins, Jacques' hair-shield grew upward to the hollow of his stomach; It wisped in long wild strands to his naval; it ran over his gaunt ribs and spread profusely over his chest. He just stood there, his shoulder haunched while his arms hung loosely at his sides.

After a while, Michael sought for a closer and clearer glance. When he saw Jacques' legs. He stiffened in cold shock!

Jacques no longer had legs. Not human legs! His thighs curved outward in arcs. They were matted with a thick wooly growth which coursed downward to boney shanks. Jacques was standing on the hind-legs of a goat.

Below then, Michael saw gray horned hooves!

# CHAPTER FIFTEEN

loven hooves.

Michael suspected those were the very hooves which had thudded outside the tower door and disappeared so mysteriously in the dark. Jacques must have been trying to return to his room to conceal his deformity; to make himself whole in order to present himself to his great-aunt.

In the mirror, Michael had seen Camille. She also was returning from somewhere, coming through the hall—possibly to keep her appointment with Jacques. Had Jacques terrible form been hiding in the black corridor, and had Michael passed him as he stumbled blindly in the dark? He remembered seeing nothing, only that he had suffered the grim feeling that something had been there watching—

Mimoutte had once sore began to flit about, dancing to as mysterious beat that only she heard. She pranced up to the jury of toads. One of them handed her a document. Mimoutte fluttered moth-like up the craggy steps. She showed the paper to Beel. A lusty leer of satisfaction burned in his eyes. He smoldered, slowing changing to a flaming magenta. Mimoutte fled to her mistress, presenting her the parchment. Camille's eager long fingers broke open the hot wax seal which Beel had just pressed. Her eyes devoured the written words. Her face lighted with victory. She flashed the contract into Jacques face.

His malformed body shrank even more; a weak cry of defeat broke in his throat as he locked haplessly upon the parchment.

Camille's full-blown body arched in triumph. She forced Jacques, who helplessly tried to resist, to accept, and to hold the decree ordering his own damnation!

"Poor Jacques!" Madame Cecile's broken voice sobbed from somewhere behind Michael.

Michael whirled around, taking his eyes from the ghastly tragedy enfolding below him, but nothing was behind him except the drifting vapors.

Mimoutte simply could not contain her Joy. She snatched the parchment so feebly held by Jacques. She fanned it before his eyes, laughing madly then danced away, brandishing the document over her head. She screeched, she floated before the jury of malignant toads.

The bloated toads began to puff and swell even more, spittle oozed from their poisonous mouths, Their great bulbous eyes quivered with excitement while ugly sounds broke from their white throats.

Beel rose before his throne. He tightened the purple mantle closer to his regal personage. His lips curled as he smiled evilly upon his subject. His face has become white-fire, wherein a pair of black eyes flamed. He nodded approvingly.

Camille would be rewarded. She felt it.

There was a moment of stifling silence. Out of the dead quietness, there thundered a raucous cry! A chorus of sadistic joy trembled the walls. The toads, with all the enmity of their slimy beings, vocally sanctioned the condemnation of Jacques.

Beel turned to his hideous Jury. The white-fire of him lighted each of the toad's faces. The light revealed their features; it told who they once were: men of history, who bartered their souls for a tyrant's power. Now, each was pitifully and hopelessly Satan's pawn.

They were famished. Never were they to drink the wind; walk in their flesh beneath stars, nor taste the rain. The holy white-wheat, which is man, nor the sweet whisper of leaves was eternally lost to them. So they hungered for the taste of Jacques soul.

They could not contain the joy of victory, refusing to be still. Their malicious jubilation grew wilder and wilder. Camille and Mimoutte humbled their persons before Sovereign Beel. Jacques merely whimpered and turned his eyes away. His spinal column was so bent that each vertebrae stood out in a hard corrugated arc.

No longer could he bear the proceeding below him, a sudden emotional explosion broke involuntarily from Michael's throat. He took hold of the poker he had carried from the room and began to beat it as hard as he could against the railing. "Stop it!" he screamed. "Stop it!" He slammed the poker again and again. The sound of the hammering of the poker and the loud eruption of his voice, surprised even Michael. He heard his voice echo and rattle up the circular chimney. He also realized that he had betrayed his presence. Silence swept the cave—necks and eyes were straining upward, shocked and stupefied but holding him fast in their gaze!

Michael yelled again, letting free all the furious and painful emotion he had been suffering. "You—And—You! Damn you!"

he screamed again, and in that same moment comprehending how useless. His sudden violence left Michael trembling.

In his rage he had forgotten caution. He rested his weight against the two-by-four railing.

The rotted wood cracked—too quickly for him to catch his balance. He fell!

His fall had slammed him so terribly hard upon his back, that he could only lie there stunned—his body writhing in pain.

For a long moment, Michael could not open his eyes. Finally he blinked and discovered that he could see across the pit to the dais. He allowed his head to fall back to the steaming floor, knowing that at least, his intrusion had disrupted the foul ceremony.

The malevolent court was stunned! The toads squatted in stark silence.

Beel had turned purple-black, his brute hulk was bent forward. He casually glanced over the boiling pond to view this interloper who had fallen upon them. Michael blinked helplessly, Beel was a monstrous, unmoving shadow silhouetted against the flames. After a moment, he relaxed. He softened into a molten-gold, calmly accepting the violent interruption.

Mimoutte stood transfixed, awaiting her master's command. Jacques had collapsed and lay sprawled at the base of the craggy steps.

Michael moaned in pain. Camille was the first to move. She turned defiantly from the dais, swinging her body in a sharp insolent twist. Her dark eyes were hard and furious. She was beside herself that anyone would dare disturb this event! Her black hair whipped behind her so that her face stood out white and sharp.

Her action gave command for the toads to move.

The toads broke silence. Hideous, angry noises came out of them. They began to waddle from their places—not only the jury, but many others. Toads emerged from all aides of the cave; materialized from the very walls.

Michael struggled to lift himself upon one elbow. He desperately tried to jerk movement into his paralyzed legs. His eyes widened as he saw Camille move closer end closer to him. Her mouth was wet; her bare arms were swinging, while her arms were outstretched. She seemed so eager to take Michael. A mass of slimy toads hopped about her feet. The humpy things also desire him. Their mouths were pursed, sucking the air—they crept with Camille toward Michael's prostrated body.

# CHAPTER SIXTEEN

amille paused and locked down at him. Michael caught a glimpse of her bare foot and the scarlet polish of her toenails. A toad, which had been just an inch before her, turned his head and leaped backwards—the next moment the toad was perched on her instep and looking at Michael.

The incident filled him with disgust.

The back of his head ached; his body was still numb and not fully under his command. For an intolerable moment he felt powerless to help himself. He was, nevertheless, gravely aware of Beel's formidable presence, of Mimoutte's startled face, and the creeping toads.

Michael lifted his eyes to Camille's face. She was hovering above him. Her pink tongue flicked through her full red lips, and her eyes held him as she reached her arms toward him. Her sweet perfume wafted and smothered him. He felt her burning touch! It seemed impossible for him not to succumb to her temptation—not to yield to anything Camille willed.

Camille bent her head closer to him. Her trembling lips and hot breath blew softly on his face. Michael's resistance ebbed; waves of hedonic desires took possession of him. In that moment he cared for nothing, not even the survival of his soul. A hunger for sensual pleasure throbbed through his body; a need for bestial gratification crept into his heart. He desired the forbidden—the carnal!

Michael understood how simple it must have been for Jacques to fall and to be captured by Camille's allure.

A faint burning feeling at the side of his mouth began to pain and distract him. He recalled that which Madame Cecile had warned: "Camille survives on the youth of men . . ." But with her smothering nearness, it was difficult for Michael to follow that warning. His head ached too much for him to think clearly. He simply longed to give in to the appealing sensual morass of unconsciousness and the licentious fleshy-dreams taking from in his brain.

A moment past—he shook his head and began to fight back to sanity. He drew in a deep breath and dragged himself from the slow, insistent current of lethargy. He pulled himself from under Camille's shadow.

She burning feeling stung again; he put his tongue to it. He tasted blood. Obviously when he fell he also cut his mouth. Camille had been looking at the blood too. He saw her pulse throbbing in her white throat. Then she shifted her eyes. Something of interest took her attention.

Michael followed the line of her gaze. Her eyes ware focused on his hand. Immediately he knew what she saw. His ring. Michael twisted his neck to see the ring. The stone was glowing. It was as bright as flame!

He recalled the legend Madame Cecile related. He wondered if it was in anyway true? Was if possible for this jewel to hold such power that it could spare Jacques, and also rescue him as well? Suddenly his eyes met Camille's eyes. He thought he saw retreat and intimidation there. Was Camille actually in fear of the cat's-eye-stone?

Michael felt his head dear. He grew in strength and began to free himself from the spell of her seduction. Camille continued to stare at his ring; her eyes were moist and soft with wonder. Watching her radiance, Michael gasped at the closeness of her. She had been that lovely girl he had dreamed of when in the tower room and he feared if he were not strong enough that he would once more fall beneath her power.

How much closer they had all had come—Camilla's lord, Beel, the fiendish Mimoutte would take him! They would assist Camille. The toads would suck his body dry of blood. He had profaned their sanctuary—frustrated their black ritual! No mortal could witness that, and escape. They would see to it! In the end, not only would they have Jacques, but him, too, in the bargain!

Something began to move along Michael's leg. It terrified him. It was a toad! First one then others. That one should touch him, filled Michael with horror. Still more came—soon they were crawling all over his body! Unable to move or protect himself. Michael screamed!

A streak of white shot out of the dark, leaping past his shoulder.

The cat!

"Kit! Oh, Kit!" he cried.

Instantly, the toads gathered. They drew off to one side, forming a semi-circle. They watched and waited for a chance to leap upon him again. But in that instant of fear, Michael felt his body break free from the force which held him. Pushing himself back against a rock, Michael got to his feet. He stomped his feet and swung his arms to get back his circulation. He prepared himself for a fight.

The cat was up on its haunches; its ears drawn back and claws extended. The cat glared at Camille. It took a stance between she and Michael while an intrepid low growl rumbled in its throat. A few toads ventured forward—the undaunted little animal turned savagely upon one, caught it in its teeth and flung the now, inert, oozing blob in defiance before Camille.

For the first time, Michael saw fear—pure fear—come into Camille's face. She and the courageous little cat were evidently old adversaries, and had met again.

Camille cowered, but in defense she extends her own strange talons. Her long, scarlet nails flashed, ready to rend and tear into the small white body. But in spite of the sudden duel with her feline enemy, Camille kept her strange burning eyes upon Michael. Eyes which flashed their bitter strange message to his heart: You wrought this!

Michael stared back. He couldn't take his eyes away as anger transformed her face. How could he had ever once thought her beautiful? Her lips had lost their fullness, they changed into a twisted, ugly jagged lines. Her angry breath hissed through her flattened nostrils. Her tongue was again showing between her teeth; spittle dripped from her chin. She was a horror!

In those ensuing moments, Michael could not tell if she was: woman—devil—or witch. He <u>did</u> know that he must destroy Camille. It was she or him!

It must be done now, he told himself. Now, while the valiant little cat had divided the attention of the forces against him. He looked around quickly. From the corner of his eye, Michael saw, close by, a sharp piece of the broken railing. He reached down and eagerly snatched the jagged wood.

He tested the balance of the wood for a good holding place. He braced his left foot against the rock in back of him. He steadied his position in the line with his target. Michael took a deep breath. He held it and for one long instant, Michael exulted in the thudding of his heart; if he failed in the action that he was about to take, his lungs would not draw breath again, his heart would not beat again.

He bit his lower lip and held it between his teeth. He tightened his grip on his primitive weapon, swiftly raising it above his head, he took aim and hurled it! Like a javelin it flew from his fingers. It flew unerringly through the air, and cut into the soft flesh of that strange Creole witch. The sharp wood pierced Camille just under her left breast.

Camille's eyes widened. They fluttered at the shock. She opened her mouth, but did not make a sound. Her long fingers reached for the wood, clutching it, hoping to free it from her heart. She began to waver, her face in pain, then she fell.

But it was the scream! The awful piercing scream which frosted Michael's blood. He thought it was Camille screaming, as naturally it should have been, but on the contrary, it was Mimoutte's voice which cut the air with that deafening cry!

A first Michael thought it was the high wailing of the cat, still battling the toads. He swung his head to see, but his attention was instantly diverted by a sudden bright light.

Where Camille had fallen, a pyre of flames was licking the air!

In a moment nothing was left or Camille but a heap of smoldering ashes, Mimoutte's terrible scream had suddenly broken off. When Michael twisted his neck to see, her scarecrow figure had disappeared. There was only a scattering of dust, drifting in the air before Beel's throne.

# CHAPTER SEVENTEEN

I t had grown darker within the cave, Michael wondered why? True, the fires were beginning to burn lower, but that was not the cause. It was Beel. The shadow of him had suddenly grown. The colossal silhouette of him, trembling in the light of the flames, fell over the walls and ground, closing Michael in, in a different kind of gloom.

Michael's horror-filled heart began to ask how was he to escape from the foul-hole he had blundered into ... How was he to fulfill his promise to Madame Cecile ... save Jacques and himself as well? He speculated if there was an exit from this lower level, or was it possible for him to make his way to the mud-steps against the wall. But that indicated that he would have to emerge into the lighted area and within the sight of Beel.

Suddenly Beel's booming laughter began to echo throughout the cave. The great sound broke above Michael's head. It was if Beel had been listen to his thoughts and was vastly amused by them.

Beel descended the craggy steps, then came forward, the jeweled pall trailing after him. The green vapors fondled his ankles in obeisance.

Michael glanced at his hand and saw that his ring was glowing. He studied the strange brightness of the stone. There was something about it that gave him courage. A strong thought swept through his head. After all, what jurisdiction had Beel over him? So Michael figured while Beel moved in one direction, he would steal about in another. This was his chance to get to the other side. However, something stopped him. He caught an image of Beel who looked strangely melancholy. Beel paused thoughtfully by the amber glow on the ground. He tilted his head sideways as if to ask of himself; was this his once beloved Camille?

Michael felt frozen on the spot. He hunched closer and listened!

Was there a whimper? Did not the ashes stir or was it merely a draft? Did he hear Camille a voice plead: "Restore me, Beel!" or was it the wind rising in the tower? He told himself: "Hold on to sanity, Mike! Hold fast."

Beel's mood changed. There was no sadness in him, no loyalty. He dipped his golden hand into the ashes. How soon they had changed, no longer aglow but gray and cold. He gathered a fistful of dust and flung it over his head. The dead ashes ignited! They sparked and fluttered aloft, mingling with the ascending vapors, flashing green and gold and fiery. Beel lifted his face to the flying sparks and laughed. His laughing breath was so full of contempt that it roared out of him powerful guffaws. It flew across the seething pit, fanning back the fires in the hollow of the toads. He drew the jeweled mantle over him, then danced away under a shower of raining drops of fire.

She gleaming ashes flew in a whirlwind about the cave and over Michael's head. Michael sniffed the air. He though that he caught the scent of cloth and burning flesh.

Suddenly Beel turned around abruptly. He sensed that Michael had moved. He saw him as he sprinted from the shadows and skirted the opposite rim of the pit.

Michael kept going. Soon his eye spotted the poker. It was lying halfway over the bank of the steaming pond. It glowed; the tip was white hot. He reached it and grabbed it up. The handle had been protected by the dank of the muddy bank. It scorched his palm, but he hardly noticed. He was too intent on keeping one eye on Beel, who was staring at him menacingly. Gradually he worked his way around the pond toward Jacques, searching all the while for a way out.

Finally he stepped backwards. He struck his heel against the bottom step and almost stumbled over Jacques' prostrated body which lay still and limp on the craggy rise.

Quickly he caught his balance and jumped to the above step. He bent over Jacques' still form, but couldn't tell if he was unconscious or dying or dead. He saw, however, that the body had neither changed nor deteriorated, evidence that Beel had not yet won!

Michael raised his eyes only to meet Beel's ghastly face. He was quite still and was simply watching him. There was, also, a curious expression in Beel's golden face. It seemed to Michael like a mixture of puzzlement and malevolence. Also, something else. Was it fear of Michael ... the very ring itself, or was curled under lip a case of simply mockery. Michael's thoughts put a dryness in his throat. "What was hold Beel in check—Why didn't he strike—take Michael with all his evil power! The heat of the flames flanking the dais was unbearable; sweat drenched Michael's clothing; it steamed down his brows into his eyes, only to trouble him. He knew he had to be brazen! A show of boldness seemed the only way to escape.

"Don't delay!" he told himself. "Move, Mike!"

He held himself straight and tall when a sudden inspiration throbbed in his heart. Beside him, lying over a big rock was Jacques' tattered shirt.

Instantly, Michael bent over the shirt and began to beat it! Striking it over and over. As he pounded on the cloth, long whelps of blood began to stain the back of the shirt. The material bled as if it were flesh. Suddenly it slipped from the rock. Blood-stained, it lay at Michael's feet—limp! It was if the shirt suffered a pardon from what evil possessed it. The silky white cross emblazoned over the pocket looked very white.

Michael could not help but look upon the shirt in wonder. At that same time he had to back up a step, he raised his eyes: Beel's monstrous shadow had crept so very close! He held fast to the poker. It was then that his free hand struck something inside his pocket. Quickly he put his hand into the pocket of his jacket.

The thoughts raced back to the crowded vestibule at Rachel's. He remembered: The Contessa has brushed against him. She had slipped something into his pocket. "You may need this!" She whispered then patted his hip.

Michael pulled out something that was cooling to his fingers. It was as large as a silver-dollar. It was a holy-medal. A beautiful piece of work—medallion in shape. A tremendous cry broke from his throat. The cry came forth in a blast. "Michael!" he cried again; "Michael!"

At once, it was both the assertion of his own identity and the battle cry in the name of the powerful Archangel.

The challenge reverberated to Beel! A sudden thought told him what to do. Jacques' twisted body was lying just beside him. He bent closer to the body. Caught it by one shoulder and turned it over on its back. Michael shook his head, Jacques' face was simply too awful to look upon. His features were matted with hair. The mouth twisted, but it was Jacques' eyes. They were wide open, horror stricken, dead and senseless, glaring back at him!

Michael trembled, His fist tightened upon the silver medallion. But it was the poker that seemed to take on a new fire. The tip glowing red!

He bent over Jacques' chest. He put the hot poker to Jacques' flesh. There he raised two blistering marks, cauterizing one horizontal—the other, vertical. The smell of scorched hair and flesh mingled with the wafting smell of sulfur. But it was done—He branded a perfect cross over Jacques' heart!

Looking up from his deed and drenched with sweat, shaking with emotion, Michael faced the ghastly image standing before him. If need be, he was ready to die.

However, it looked to Michael that Beel had back up. He was too dazed to think clearly but it seemed so. Beel was looking at something . . . he seemed to be cowering. Michael turned his glance to the poker. A bright glow came from it. It looked to be shining in the form of a cross. The light from the poker threw forth long shafts of pure white, dazzling light!

Michael felt that he must speak . . . say something, no matter what, in defense of Jacques as well as himself. His lips trembled. He didn't know what he should say. However words came. His first thought was to throw the medallion toward Beel. He did. Whispering: "Michael! . . . Michael!"

"In the name of God . . . The almighty. You are commanded to release and deliver-up this soul!"

An inhuman sound; a growl responded: "Who dares to challenge His Satanic Highness!"

Michael lifted the poker. The magnificent rays reached Beel. He was advancing upon Michael, but he stopped. He seemed to have weakened. However, he was not finished, bluffing Michael with his earth-shaking laughter, wishing to undermine that newfound courage.

Beel lifted his power arm as if to strike out at Michael, but as he did so, he also crept backward seeking the security of the dais and his altar. Beel's figure seemed to be fading as he stood before his throne. For a moment he was hidden behind smoke and vapors. When all cleared another figure was standing before Michael. The entity said in a gentle voice:

"Would you, dear boy, hurt your Monsignor, Mike . . . ?" Michael could not believe his eyes. He knew the voice; he recognized the fine rounded head; the complexion with its florid pinkness and the sparse white hair of his Monsignor from school days.

The sight of the gentle old man thrilled Michael's heart. For a second he actually believed he saw his faithful friend. But his monsignor had been dead for years.

A wild and bitter laugh rancored in Michael's breast.

"Oh, ho! Ho! Satanic Highness!" Michael cried mockingly. "What pitiful bluff. No! You are no monsignor of mine. You are defeated—Jacques' body is still the temple of The Holy Ghost." And although the cry was ancient; it was perfectly suitable to the cause . . . Michael himself trembled at speaking them! "You are defeated . . . The simple cross has beaten you . . . Weep for that which you yourself have lost . . . And, lost forever, Lucifer!"

Suddenly Beel grew Blacker than ever. He made a final attempt at intimidating Michael. Beel roared with laughter until the walls and the earth itself trembled under Michael's foot. A strange shadow began to move toward Michael. He felt certain that whatever it was, that it would fold him into its blackness and take him!

"No!" screamed Michael. "You have lost! Lost!" He lifted the poker brandishing the light. "See for yourself!"

The jury of toads and the others as well had disappeared. The flames in the stone replicas had gone out. A soft breeze drifted through the cave. Jacques' face was lighted by the dwindling fires surrounding the pond. His face had changed completely. His features returned to normal. His handsome mouth relaxed. His body; his malformed limbs changed back to man's. He was whole. He was at peace.

Beel looked on in defeat. He drew the mortuary cloth closer about him. However the folds of the cloth lacked substance. It appeared as if nothing or no one was within it; that it ms limp; that it only seemed to be a head and shoulders.

Michael believed that the huddled mass was coning at him. But no. It was drifting toward the edge of the pool. Then the cloth looked as if it was sinking, seeming to fall lower and lower, until finally, it dropped and lay in the drifting vapors. He lifted the poker somewhat higher, but even with that he could not see too clearly, for even the light from the poker was beginning to fade. However, Michael knew that his prayer for help had been answered, that was the greatness of the moment.

Soon darkness was beginning to creep upon him, when a sudden and tremendous bolt of lightning crashed out of the storm and split the heavens. The ground trembled under him, and when he looked up, he saw that another bolt had struck the tower! Orange fingers of fire began to tear into the blackness above.

But Beel was gone.

Only the purple cloth lay upon the steps, trailing into the pond. From one of its folds, a half-hidden jewel winked.

# CHAPTER EIGHTEEN

I t was a strange, swift interval.

Beel was gone!

At once, Michael's brain was both numb and reeling with relief. But he knew through the strain of it all, that it was only the Grace of God that saved him and brought peace to Jacques' soul. But in some way, he had been the Lord's Grenadier, in spite of his doubting.

Filled with gladness, Michael lifted his eyes to the tower and to the flames consuming it. Suddenly there began a grinding and Michael slipped and wobbled—the step beneath his feet swayed and rocked. It was as if Beel was underground, beating and tearing the foundation under him in frustrated anger. He feared the ground would open and swallow him. The fiery tower looked as if at any moment it might collapse into the pit.

The trembling moved and shook the purple cloth so that its folds fell open and revealed a blazing array of gems. Instinctively, Michael wanted to reach, out and touch them, but the inner-man within his soul cautioned him! He leaped off the steps. On the ground near his feet were a few strips of wood. He gathered two strips and laid them in the form of a cross over Jacques' nude and lifeless body. Michael heaved a breath of wonder as he swayed his head, for he could see the tranquility which had come to the man.

He gave a last desperate glance to his surroundings, and of course to the extravagant purple cloth sprawled there in front of him. The great beauty and nearness of it simply commanded him to look. He could not very well keep his eyes off of the cloth. A heap of glittering wealth lay within reach of his fingers! Pearls rolled toward him and trickled at his feet like drops of dew. A suggestion rattled in his heart; "Why not . . . It is yours for the taking . . . who would know!"

A hysterical laugh shook Michael's weary body. It was just Beel's style to stir-up covetousness and temptation in his wake. One touch would negotiate a fatal contract!

"Oh, ho! Ho!" Michael cried gaily wiping sweat from his sight. "But, mais non! Good sir!" Suddenly Michael spun about fearfully. He sensed something close by! He sensed it surely. "Back to your hell, fiend!"

Michael felt that he was not merely speaking for himself, but for Madame Cecile and Jacques as well. He turned away, seeking his way toward the steps when he saw something shining in the gloom. The St. Michael medallion. His fingers pounced upon it. He made a wild run for the mad steps.

The yawning mouth of the tower filled with smoke. A sudden, blackness swept ever him. Midway up the steps, Michael paused and looked down. The pool was slowly closing; its circle of diminishing light seemed that it, too, had paused to look back at Michael. To Michael, the mystic pool, looked like an eye; <u>Green and Watching</u>!

He felt his way along the dank wall. "Finally he struck the toe of his shoe against the ledge, causing him to stumble forward and he bumped his head on the low arch. Gleefully, he welcomed this new and small hurt. It was a signpost in the gloom. He bobbed under the arch. He recalled that the passage ahead of him was straight. He saw a square shape of light way ahead of him. His heart made a little jump. He knew that it was the opening of the old fireplace. But something looked wrong! Fear touched him. The sides of the fireplace seemed to be moving together. He thought it would close. The faster he ran, the longer the passage seemed. His legs felt-heavy and his back began to ache from his fall.

In desperation Michael flung himself face downward. He forced his body to move the rest of the way. He reached the crack just in time to stop it from closing. He thrust the poker into the crack, then pulled it back as if it were an oar.

He braced his back against one side of the stone panel, bringing his knees up to his chest, so that the bottom of his shoes against the other side. He renewed his breath; straightened his body, pushing with all of his strength, until he forced the plates backwards.

Losing his balance, Michael fell over on his side and rolled into the dust of the dead ashes. He laid halfway on the hearth until he could extricate himself from the bricked recess of the chimney. For a long second he found himself marooned on the carpet. When he lifted his eyes he saw smoke seeping through the papered ceiling. A crack of fire flickered through—Soon the entire ceiling burst into flame!

Michael jumped to his feet. He fled to the great arch, only to find the corridor in flames—the staircase burning! The window was his only exit. In a spasm of energy, Michael violently ripped the heavy draperies from their massive brass rod. It was an effort to lift the heavy large window. He pounded upon it, when he at last he broke it free, the frame cracked, the sash-corc screeched, crying on the downward plunge of the weights. The slip-latch of the ancient cypress blinds would not give. He lifted his foot; he kicked them through. The howl of the wet wind swept strongly against his body. One whistling gust after another lashed him, blowing into his face, slipping into his clothes. He welcomed it. It was a relief and restored his vigor.

Making ready to jump, he paused resting one knee on the window sill. Michael turned his glance into the room. He saw Madame's chair.

Her chair was overturned. It seemed strangely unhappy, lying on its side as though it had been whipped. Michael's heart could not bear to leave it as such. He strode back to the chair. He knew it was foolish and sentimental of him . . . Absurd and presumptuous when flames were falling and smoke billowing through the arch, but at the moment, it was the only right thing to do.

Michael righted the chair, taking time to set it upon its carved and ornate feet. He retrieved Madame's embroidery things from the carpet and placed them over one arm of the chair respectfully. There he stood with deep-set eyes thoughtfully beside the chair, resting his hand on its high back, wishing to comfort the spirit which once possessed it.

Crackling fingers of fire crawled greedily over the ceiling and wall; but still Michael remained steadfast beside the chair; a decided purpose in mind. He said reverently: "In the presence of the Heavenly Court, peace has come to him, Madame. I'm sure! Eternal peace . . . to you and yours!"

Michael put his fingers to his lips then touched a light kiss to the back of the chair.

He turned abruptly and eased himself from the window, down to the sodden garden.

The trembling glow of the burning house and its tower flaming gave a rust-like tint to the thin, slanted rain.

Michael tore open his shirt and let the rain strike his chest. He inhaled the fragrance of the drenched and dripping trees. He sighed and all but cried for it was a reprieve from the horror he suffered. It was manna. The wet air chilled him. Un unexplainable joy possessed him and he deliberately splashed his feet in a puddle.

Excitedly, Michael turned from Fournier house and made a streak for the woods. Suddenly a gentle, pleading cry stopped him. He turned around to see the little cat. When Michael stopped, the cat stopped too. She set down upon the path and curled her tail about her forelegs. A beseeching looked appeased in the little creature's eyes as if to remind Michael that something had been forgotten.

"Yes, old friend," he said gently. He kneeled upon the path, und this time the cat allowed him to stroke her head. Michael took his ring from his finger, then got the matching stone from his pocket. The thin stone gleamed within his palm, "there you are . . ." He said and rolled the golden gems toward her, "Take them to wherever they must be—To Madame. Wherever! But they are yours." He gave her a final pat! "Thanks, Kit— Thank you!"

A satisfied purr came from her throat. She blinked and sat there quite satisfied, the stones at her feet.

Michael turned away, his eyes moist with affection for the cat which so befriended him.

He went on finding his way under the thick trees. Once he looked back. The house was not to be seen—not even a wisp of smoke.

A fresh wind sent the clouds scudding. His lips tasted the wet morning air and the breeze carried the distant sound of the parish bells.

# CHAPTER NINETEEN

The forgone weather bad left an unquestionable chill in its path—particularly for a late afternoon in May. A dancing breeze blew out of the north and sent the leaves flying in a whirlwind of delight. Its sweeping zephyrs frolicked with the generous folds of the Capuchin-style cape that Contessa Lucrezia Millano Zinadelli was wearing and filled it with air, until she looked like a balloon—a very zeppelin. She had to hold tightly to the large brimmed hat flopping about her head as the wind blew she and her buckled oxfords up the walk to Michael and Velia's door where she gingerly pressed the buzzer.

The glossy dark head of a somewhat, but beautifully attired Velia opened the door. Her expression a little surprised by the large hatted and bundled figure there.

"Goodness, Velia . . . Admit me! Admit me before this wind blows me right back to St. Martinsville."

"Lulu . . . is that you!"

"Why so surprise? You knew I was on my way. Paul dropped me, after putting down Betty and Rachel at N0. 1 Canal Place . . . they are also headed for Holmes. We made a veritable chauffer out of him. Hope he isn't mad." The Contessa paused by the console. She glance at her reflection in the mirror. "Oh, my!" she screeched. "Little wonder you were startled. I look like the Phantom of the Opera!" She laughed gaily then removed her hat. "I didn't expect this chill. I put all my things away,"

Velia replied. "You look marvelous. And, I love your mystique. Always did."

"Which brings us to your young husband. How is he? I warned him, I really did, Velia, but I guess he thought I was a mad woman."

"Well . . . I don't know what he thinks now. But for heaven sakes do not suggest a doctor or a priest. He'll kill you."

"—And, you told me over the phone that he went back there."

"Yes. He said he could not even find a stone or a piece of charred wood. All simply vanished. He even searched the papers but no fires of that kind was recorded. He declares it was all like a terrible dream, but knows it wasn't."

"I am not surprised. Nether should you. Ancient New Orleans is infested with such strangeness, Gris-gris and rites. Who know what is forgotten. What is covered over. Who know what this house is built over . . . Was not all this land, one time, Fournier estate?"

Her grim observation, gave Velia a profound turn. She lifted her shoulders in a sharply apprehensive way, seeming to shiver, then closed her eyes until her long, fringed lashes almost touched her cheek. "Really Lulu," she cried. "I have to live here, you know!"

"Darling—Sorry." She responded seeing Velia's pallid face. "I didn't mean to scare you. But you know what I meant."

She thought it prudent to say something cheerful: "How stunning you look in that hostess-gown! You certainly know how to dress." She slipped her arm around Velia's waist. The sumptuous gown that was blue and vermillion with splashes of gold leaves crackled as she drew her close. How you resemble your mother, just now." She toss her head back, squeezing the girl with reminiscence. "How I wish it were 1938, again! I see your mother and me aboard, the Ile De trance, sailing for South Hampton—Mary and I had a terrible crush on Hotsy D'Angelo, then!" She chuckled as she released Velia from her embrace. "I must see Michael." she declared quite seriously. "I've found something." There was stress in her voice. "I must show it to him."

Arm in arm they strolled to the back of the house, to the den. A spacious octagonal chamber, paneled in soft olive, having a thin gold trim. It was beautifully furnished: satinwood bookcases, leather chairs, a good painting, or two, and a worthy collection of memorabilia. Here and there, colorful, Persian throw-rugs adorned the polished wood floor. There was an oversized fireplace, flanked by long garden doors that looked out upon the fountain and scanning to invite the outdoors in. When entering, one assumed at once, a sense of peace and comfort.

The wind began to sing a bit higher as it tumbled the temperature somewhat lower. Michael could no longer suffer the chill. Fitfully he wiggled from his chair and started a blaze under the narrow logs in the fireplace. He crouched before the hearth, blowing breath upon the struggling smoke until, at last, it flared into flame.

He spent some time looking the door-panes and upon the wind-shook world. Long fingers of clouds streaked across the heavens; flying westward with the flush of the downing sun. Suddenly, there flew-up, from the white blossoms of the bridal wreath, a swarm of butterflies, winging in instant dips, circling in fancy drills, then they flitted nervously back to kiss the blossoms, whose tremulous branches could hardly bear the weight of their beauty.

After awhile of just looking and thinking, Michael suddenly placed his fingers to his eyelids. He lingered there and did not hear the approaching footsteps of Velia and the Contessa.

Velia stopped abruptly. The look of him with bowed head troubled her. She didn't understand if the gesture was to imprison the pleasantry of the garden and wind-blown sky, or if it was to escape same fearful memory. She spoke in a bright voice hoping to conceal her fear.

"Michael—look who's here!"

"Oh," Michael said softly as he turned to face them, "It's my old girl friend, Lulu."

A smile lighted her wonderful aristocratic face as she affectionately answered Michael. After her long conversation with Velia she well understood what he must have suffered. She said: "Am I truly your girl friend, Michael . . . really? I so want to be."

"Wasn't it you who slipped St. Michael into my pocket?"

"Guilty—sir."

"Then you are my girl friend."

"You wouldn't tease an old lady would you, Michael."

"I won't . . . If you won't look at my aura."

"You darling scoundrel!" she shrieked while a gentle laugh trembled in her breast, "But I dad caution you."

"What now?"

"Only goodness and happiness with this lovely girl!"

The last rays of the sun faded into twilight, and from the garden blue shadows of evening crept in, darkening the room. A soft wind in the flu caused the fire to crackle as its ribbons of smoke, rimmed with white lire curled up the chimney.

Michael sauntered over to a large leather chair. He was dressed in creams-colored trousers and a white v-neck sweater. The light from the table lamp in the center of the room fell mellowly upon him casting his nose and fine mouth and well cut chin into easy view. Velia looked lovingly upon her husband. She did not realize before how completely his blue eyes so dominated his whole aspect. She thought: His eyes are blue-fire, indeed. She looked at his long frame as he settled himself rather wearily into the great chair. She went over to him, wishing to sit on the arm of his chair. Suddenly, Michael pulled her into his lap, mussing his face against her breast, folding her into his arms and drawing her tightly to his body.

Velia felt the throb of him against her! A delicate, sweeping dilemma of warmth and affection left her somewhat perplexed. She turned halfway in his arms her hand resting on his chest as she could feel his heart striking against her palm. Velia blushed unable to free herself from his strength. Her quandary being, too, that Lulu was there.

"Ah! L'amour" Lulu cried clapping her hands together. "L'amour!" She spread out her arms, then moved about making a kind of waltzing steps. Her pink mails called attention to her singularly broad, large knuckled hands where an enormous emerald flashed. For a second the tall graceful rounded woman stood still, gazing at the young couple, her dreamy eyes smiling affectionately.

"You—romantic old darling," cried Velia. "For that, you may fix the drinks!"

"You haven't addressed me like that since you were a child." She dropped her arms down to her ample thighs. "I am not a drinking woman—But today, I need a drink! I've had something of a startling afternoon myself."

She went to the oblong table against the wall where an antique, Dutch silver spirit-case stood open holding some siphons of soda-water and some large glass tumblers. Also on that table was a garment-box from a gentlemen's shop. A handsome blue velvet jacket lay on top the box. "how beautiful, Velia—Lucky boy, Michael to have it!" Lulu returned to their side bearing the drinks expertly. She paused momentarily and gazed into the bright wood fire. She replied: "L'amour . . . Tojour, L'amour!" She took a sip of the drink and grimaced. "Yes! I deliberately made them strong. We will need it. Listen . . . I have spent the better part of the morning rummaging through the old newspaper morgue—Where is my handbag? Oh, here, here!" Her hand searched into the large, cloth bag and she took from it a photo-copy of an old newspaper item. She studied it, gave a heavy sigh then extended the paper. "Read this, Velia—"

The copy was fancifully boxed in lacy black ink and framed with lacy curlicues, a style favored by editors of that day:

## City Loses Architectural Treasure

Fire of undetermined origin has claimed Historical Fournier House! Officials said the blaze occurred during the early hours this morning. It is believed the holocaust was begun by an electrical storm which swept the city. The splendid bayou mansion was constructed in the early years of the century by the noted public benefactor and distinguished merchant-prince, Louis Fournier. Founder of: Fournier & Beluche, House of imports, Inc., No. 12 Rue Royal. The present owner is, Mlle. Camille Fournier, who at this time is enjoying a European sojourn. Inspector Gaston Maseau promises a speed investigation, but can not account for the deposits of sulfur discovered in the ruins.

———————

The article was dated: 1, May, 1896

———————

## The End

# ~EPILOGUE~

Michael stretched his body full length
in the warm bath water ... Singing and splashing away
the grime of gardening and spreading soil.

He slipped under the water, bobbed up, wide-eyed.
Did he hear voices drifting from the front entrance?
"Lou-Lou?"

Presently, Velia burst in.
She screeched at the water splashed on the floor.

"Michael! Aunt Lou-Lou brought you a gift."
She brought forth,
a white kitten.

Maurice Frisell, December 20, 2010